HD

Having previously worked as a banker, Mark Neilson went on to become an Economics lecturer at Strathclyde University. He later became a consultant but is now a full-time writer.

THE VALLEY OF THE VINES

Sophie Hargreaves hopes to repair her shattered family by buying a rundown vineyard in Piedmont and bringing everyone together again. Sadly, her attempt fails and she's left struggling to bring in the grape harvest on her own before she faces ruin. Then, just as she begins to lose hope, Sophie finds help from an unlikely source: three strangers fleeing a storm and its flooding. They find themselves wrestling with the problems of saving the grapes and making the ancient winery viable. Unexpectedly, Sophie finds a new life in the remote wine valleys of Northern Italy.

MARK NEILSON

THE VALLEY OF THE VINES

Complete and Unabridged

ULVERSCROFT
Leicester

First published in Great Britain in 2010 by
Robert Hale Limited
London

First Large Print Edition
published 2011
by arrangement with
Robert Hale Limited
London

The moral right of the author has been asserted

British Library CIP Data

Neilson, Mark.
   The valley of the vines.
   1. Families- -Fiction. 2. Wineries- -Italy- -Piedmont- -
   Fiction. 3. Piedmont (Italy)- -Fiction.
   4. Large type books.
   I. Title
   823.9'2–dc22

   ISBN 978–1–44480–599–4

Published by
F. A. Thorpe (Publishing)
Anstey, Leicestershire
Set by Words & Graphics Ltd.
Anstey, Leicestershire
Printed and bound in Great Britain by
T. J. International Ltd., Padstow, Cornwall

Acknowledgements

The longer this list, the less likely it will be read: however, I owe a huge debt of gratitude to the following.

Firstly, and most important, the many busy wine producers who took time to show me round their vineyards, cellars and even kitchens while they answered patiently my endless questions on making wine. Secondly, my wonderful interpreter Simona, who acted as our go-between and finished each night in urgent need of a throat spray; but only after she had driven me many miles along narrow roads and through tiny villages, with good humour and Italian panache. Thirdly, the Office of Tourism in Alba, who organized my research trip and my interpreter. Fourthly, the kindly consortium of local businesses who unexpectedly paid for my accommodation, while in Alba, reducing my bank manager (and myself) to tears of gratitude.

Finally, I want to thank two wonderful editors: my ex-agent Anthea Morton-Saner, who encouraged me to write — and rewrite — the original book; and Karen Byrom, who helped me restructure this into the serial on which this current version of the book is based. From the bottom of my heart, thank you, ladies.

As an addendum, there is a wine producer who fielded Simona and myself in falling snow, showed us her cellars, and sat us down in the kitchen which I have stolen for Sophie in the book, then said through Simona: I have answered your questions for an hour; now I have one of my own . . . what is this story of yours about? After I outlined the plot which was still taking shape in my mind, she started crying and said: that was my story — it happened to me.

To this real-life Sophie: one day, somehow, I will find a way to take back the bottle of wine you gave me and which I kept to mark a debt of honour — together with a copy of 'your' story. That debt is now paid: and, PS, the bottle is now empty . . .

1

The Italian morning sun shone through a golden haze of heat. It highlighted the rolling hills of the Langhe, leaving the valleys in cool purple shadows. Below her, in the distance, a dog barked. Around her, the tangy smell of cedars. Once Sophie had stood here, and thought that Heaven must surely be like this.

Now she wasn't sure. She bit her lip and glanced at the crisp letter in her hand, more conscious of its threat than of the glorious day around her. She checked her watch: barely 7 a.m., back in London. But she couldn't wait another moment.

Turning on her heel, she marched up the slope from the vines, where the grapes were almost ready for harvesting, back to the courtyard and the old villa set on top of the ridge. In the sun, the villa's amber walls and terracotta roof almost glowed. Wisteria climbed — or, rather, rioted — up into the pantiles. She must borrow a ladder and cut it back before the winter's rain and snow got through the disturbed tiles. But borrow from whom? She had no friends left in the valley — not after Brian had driven them away. And she had no money to hire a man to do the job, which should have been his to do.

She loved that old house and its cool cobbled courtyard. Had seen it as a chance to attempt what others only dreamed about: starting a new life, doing something, being someone, entirely different. This was the house that should have held her family, the house where she would one day bring her grandchildren.

Now, it was like her bank account, quite empty.

Sophie didn't do self-pity. She pushed through a kitchen door that was seldom locked, went through the shadowed kitchen with its stone slab floor, into the hallway beyond. Walking briskly to the phone, she lifted it and dialled. Waited, as it rang out in distant London, taking a long, deep breath. This part of her life was over, but she and Brian still had things in common. Like their two girls.

'Hello?' It was Brian. Who, in another life, had been her husband.

'Sophie here,' she said firmly.

A defensive pause. 'Hi,' he said. Flatly, with no emotion. Almost like he would play a hand of cards. It hadn't always been like that between them.

'I have a letter, from the girls' school,'

Sophie said. 'The term fees haven't been paid yet. You promised me you would see to that.'

'Uh-uh.' She could sense the bright and racing mind at the other end of the line, and wondered bitterly what new lies it would produce. 'A bit of a problem here,' Brian finally said. 'Cashflow hitch, that's all. I've a lot of deals at a crucial stage right now. Payment was delayed on one of them, that's my problem. It's perfectly safe and will bring mega-profits. When I get the money, I can pay the bill. Can you handle this yourself, in the meantime, if the school are getting stroppy?'

'As in threatening to send them home,' Sophie said. 'Boarding-schools don't get stroppier than that. It's only the girls' good records that are saving them. And no, I can't pay the bill. I won't have money until I get the grapes in and make the wine. Then sell it. You know that. The vineyard was drowning in debt when you gave it to me in the settlement.'

A long, expensive silence. 'If you could screw the money out of the Alba bank,' he said finally. 'Use the vineyard, or the villa, as security . . . '

'I'm mortgaged to the hilt. I can't even pay to hire men from the town to harvest the grapes. I'm going to have to do it all myself.

I'll never be able to harvest enough before the grapes grow too soft. I'm facing ruin. The bank know the situation — they're my advisers. They've frozen my credit. They're even suggesting that I should sell the place to raise funds and pay off my debts. There's absolutely no chance that they will give me enough to pay the school fees. That's the bottom line, as you would say.'

Sophie couldn't keep the bitter sarcasm from her voice.

Another, even longer silence. 'OK,' Brian said. 'Then it's down to me. I'll try to shuffle stuff, unload some assets. It's a bad time in the markets. Unloading equals loss. But I'll find a way to raise enough cash to pay the school. Trust me.'

The line went dead. As the marriage had done, many years ago. The grind of working the vineyard had never been the cause, only the occasion, of their break-up. But during the months they had struggled together to rebuild the old vineyard and winery, she had seen another side of Brian. Weakness, where she needed strength and decision; arrogance, when she needed someone willing to dirty his hands and learn from the valley people, who had been happy to help.

It was as if the bright city high-flier she had married had burned out in a brilliant flame, leaving only cinders. That pained her. Once they had been happy; they had made and brought up two wonderful girls together. Then, Brian's wit and energy had been their driving force. Suddenly, it had gone like the love they had once felt for one another. That love had been real, but life changed people. It had changed Brian, changed both of them. There was no laughter in her now: she was a driven, obsessive woman. Without the harvest, and the wine this year, she was ruined.

Sophie set the phone onto its cradle gradually aware that someone was watching. It was Maria, her home-help from the village who looked after the old house and cooked for them. Because, working from dawn to dusk on the vineyard, there was never any time.

'*Buongiorno, signora.*' The older woman looked troubled.

How much of the conversation had she overheard, Sophie wondered?

'*Buongiorno, Maria.*'

Suddenly, the air was thick with tension, when she already had all the worry she could handle. Sophie sighed. 'I'm going out to the slopes to look at the grapes again,' she said. 'When are the valley people harvesting this year?'

'The Barbero and Dolcetto grapes are

already in. The Nebbiola, maybe in four days' time . . . maybe a week. It depends on the weather. My sons say that a big storm is coming.' Maria spoke in the local *patois* of French and Italian, used by the people in these remote Piemonte valleys. Sophie's language now. After three years here, she dreamed in it more often than in English. She had gone native and was too busy to be bothered. Once these natives had been her closest friends.

Maria stared at her, troubled black eyes in a dark, sun-wrinkled face.

'How are you bringing in the harvest, *signora*?' she asked quietly.

'By myself,' Sophie answered grimly.

'Not men from the city like last year? When they knew so little and worked so fast, they damaged half the grapes. And ruined your wine.'

'I will be more careful.'

'One person only, to bring in four hectares of harvest? In the two, maybe three days when the grapes are ready?' Maria asked. 'It is impossible.'

'Then I will do the best I can,' said Sophie.

She turned away, but not before she saw Maria shake her head.

★ ★ ★

The old couple leaned against the ship's rail, wind from the ferry's passage streaming through the woman's silver hair.

'Is that France yet, Bert?' she asked.

Bert couldn't see for tears streaming down his cheeks.

Mary glanced up. 'Don't tell me you're homesick already,' she said.

'It's the wind.' Impatiently, Bert scrubbed his eyes. 'Could be France,' he said. 'Or maybe it's just a cloud.'

'Now I know how Columbus felt,' she groaned.

'But he was heading west.'

'East, west . . . what's the difference? Bet he still had a first mate who said 'mebbes aye, and mebbes naw', to every question.'

'Well, he got there, didn't he?' Bert said reasonably.

Mary's smile faded. 'I wonder if David will,' she said.

'All he's got to do is find Glasgow Airport. They'll do the rest.'

But Bert was a lot less confident than he sounded. Their only son had strangely lost his way, after his wife had been killed in the car crash. Four years later, the boy still hadn't moved on.

He seemed to have lost all ambition, drive. Not right, for a man still in his early forties.

His promising academic career had stalled. This American research trip could provide the final push he'd need to make it to professor. But Bert would be surprised if David ever made the trip. More likely to drift, find excuses, let the opportunity pass. Something he would never have done before Maureen's death.

After forty-five years of marriage, Mary could read his mind. Time to change the subject, she thought. 'Are you excited about the trip?' she asked.

'Scared.'

'Yes, I know. But don't you feel excited too? We're on the brink of the Great Adventure. The new life we've been planning and working towards for years.'

'Right,' said Bert.

'We're reinventing ourselves. Making our own destiny. We've sold the house in Edinburgh, and bought our first-ever decent campervan. Now we're off to travel where the fancy takes us. Escape the Scottish winters by heading off to the Algarve every year. Then follow the spring up through Spain and France. Explore every corner of Northern Europe when the sun down south gets too hot for us. We'll follow the wind, like gypsies. See the world, while we're still fit enough to wander through it. Then go back home and buy another house, to settle down in when we're really old. Away from Edinburgh and its traffic. Maybe up north, in a fishing village — or maybe in some foreign town we've still to find . . . '

'I'll settle for finding my way out of Calais,' Bert said. 'We should have bought that sat nav — '

'You've got me, instead.'

Bert opened his mouth, then closed it. Ten years of part-time touring in a series of rusting campervans had taught him that Mary's navigation skills could barely find the nearest retail park. He was dreading finding himself in a foreign town, on the wrong side of the road, half of France, or Italy, climbing over them while Mary turned the map upside down and said, 'I think we're *here*. Turn left . . . no, right . . . just follow that car in front, in case he's going there . . . '

Any marriage that could survive Mary's directions was built on solid rock.

'Kelly thinks we're mad,' he said. Kelly was their grand-daughter and the apple of his eye. Together with her grandparents, they were the Three Musketeers, standing firm together, ready to take on the world. That left him with two bosses, and no responsibility to do anything other than what he was told.

'Don't you believe it. She envies us,' Mary said.

'She's got her Master's to do, this year,' Bert objected.

'After being President of the Students' Union?' Mary asked.

'What's that got to do with it?'

'Everything. It's shown her that there's a big world out there beyond the university walls. She's going to find it hard, to settle down.'

'She's got the brains for it,' Bert argued. 'Being an academic, like her dad.'

'She knows she wasn't cut out for that life,' Mary said quietly. 'She's a doer, a fighter for lost causes. Not a bloodless academic.'

'Oh,' said Bert. Another dream crumbling.

Mary shielded her eyes. 'I'm sure that's France,' she said. 'I can't wait to get started. Out onto the open road. Braid flowers in my hair.'

'What flowers?' said Bert. 'It's October.'

'Then buy me flowers,' Mary sighed. 'Use your imagination.'

'Right,' he said, his arm reaching out to lie across her shoulder.

With all his heart, he wished he'd spent more time memorizing his route before turning Mary loose on Europe. Would it ever be the same again — Europe, that is. Did it know what was coming to it, in the form of one old Scottish lady?

Sophie glanced at the leaden sky. Another heavy drop of rain splashed onto her upturned face. Maria's sons had been right: a storm was coming and from the black clouds which engulfed even the low hills of the Langhe, it would be a bad one.

Her face was stained green by chemicals from the vines' foliage, with white channels worn by sweat. She leaned against a trellis post, panting, and dropped the empty plastic crate at her feet. Her legs quivered. For two days and most of a night, she hadn't slept, but had thrown herself mindlessly at the challenge of getting the grapes in before the fruit over-ripened, clipping the dark purple cones of grapes, and laying them into the plastic crates she dragged behind her.

She could never cut enough grapes to make a commercial harvest. The task was impossible for any single person. There simply wasn't time. To make matters worse, her small tractor had broken down and lay useless in its workshed up in the villa courtyard leaving her to drag and carry the fruit up to the cellars, to be pressed. Each full crate of grapes weighed heavier than an airport suitcase and each had to be wrestled up the steep vineyard slope, along the track, then stacked in the cellars, waiting to be pressed overnight.

The trip took a bare five minutes at the start of each day but nearer twenty by the end of it. Without that tractor, she was spending more time carrying than harvesting. She didn't have the technical know-how to repair it although she'd tried her best. And she didn't have either the money, or the credit, to bring a mechanic up from Alba to do the job for her. She had no friends left in the valley, small growers who would surely have been able to do something to get the brute going.

Sophie was exhausted, sweaty. As she leaned her head against the trellis post, her eyes filled up. She scrubbed at them angrily with the back of a vine-stained hand, rearranging the chemicals — and white channels — on her face.

Then her shoulders firmed. She didn't do failure. She would go on until she dropped and struggle to bring in enough grapes to make enough wine to pay off even part of the debt which had accrued on the old vineyard — her dream of a new future which had become a living nightmare.

'*Signora*, you must not cut the grapes when rain is falling.'

Sophie looked wearily up to the top of the ridge. It was Maria.

'The rainwater will spoil the wine. Dilute the grape juice.'

'I know,' said Sophie.

'You haven't eaten. You haven't slept. Not in three days.'

'I can eat and sleep when this is done.'

'Where is the sense, *signora*? Harvesting needs many hands.'

'Two hands are better than none.' Sophie's will was like iron.

The older woman hesitated, then came carefully down the slope. Grey cardigan over a charcoal-grey thick skirt, her dark grey stockings were wrinkled around her ankles. Standard dress for the older local women.

Sophie steadied her as she slipped. 'Careful,' she said. Then realized that Maria was crying. Silent tears, from eyes which wouldn't meet her own. 'What is the matter, Maria?' she asked quietly. 'What has happened?'

'It is my sons.'

'Has something happened to them?'

A silent shake of the head.

'Then what's wrong?'

'They say that I must not work for a woman who cannot pay me.'

The words carried the power of a slap across Sophie's face. 'But,' she said, 'I have always paid you . . . '

13

'I told them that. But they say you are finished. Last year, a harvest where the grapes were bad. This year, your grapes are good but will rot on the vines. Your husband has gone. The bank is ready to foreclose. You are ruined. My sons say I must leave before we are both embarrassed. I do not want to leave you, but . . . '

Sophie had believed she could not possibly feel worse. Wrong. Maria had been a prop to her in the early months. A cheerful, sensible, mother figure around the house. To lose her, like this, was the final blow. The ultimate rejection. 'I would have gone without myself before I did not pay you,' she protested.

'You already have, *signora*. Perhaps it is for the best.' Maria's tears were flowing freely. 'I have left some food in the kitchen for you. Please, with all my heart, stop this senseless punishment. Go up and eat it. Then take some sleep. The storm is almost on us. There is nothing you can do while rain is falling. Only the Old Ones can save you now . . . '

The valley people lived in rural isolation, following an almost pagan blend of religion and superstition. When they had just taken over the vineyard, she had asked Sergio, their neighbour up the valley, who the Old Ones were. His weathered face creased into a smile. 'The ancients,' he explained. 'The timeless custodians of the vines. Vines have been grown on these slopes since the Roman Empire was the only civilization in the world. There is a presence in these old places — we call it the spirit of the vines. The watching shadow left by all the people who have loved the place and spent their lives working its slopes. A benign spirit, not one from the Devil. It was they who made you turn off the wine road on that holiday with your family. They spoke to you. Recognized the next custodian of their vines, the person to take over the most precious place on Earth.'

His smile became an impish grin. 'But you, a twenty-first-century sophisticate from London will never believe an ancient tale like this. I would not expect it.'

First Sergio: now Maria. She missed all the rough and ready small growers who had once dropped in when they were passing, to show her how to do the different chores in growing vines. They had become her friends, as well as mentors, until Brian's arrogance and pig-headed actions had driven them away.

As they had probably driven off the Old Ones too. Sophie glanced up at the sky. It pressed on her, heavy as her worries.

'I'll stop, in a moment,' she said dully. 'Let me try to fill this crate before the rain sets in.'

'I knew we should have turned right at Calais,' Bert said dismally.

'Think of all that lovely rain we would have missed,' Mary replied.

She clutched at Bert, as their bed rocked in the van, and the wind howled round them once again, driving huge drops of heavy rain against the side and roof of the van. Sleep was impossible: this was like living inside a kettledrum.

'We're safe enough,' he said. 'Better than being caught out on these Italian motorways, on a night like this.

'Where are we?' she asked.

'You're the navigator. I thought you were Columbus.'

'Well, it's not America. Trust me on that.'

Bert winced, as another squall howled down the valley and sent the big van reeling, like a ship moored in a storm. The drumming of rain rose to a crescendo.

'What about that river, running through the site?' Mary asked.

'That's why I pitched up here. As far from the river as I could get.'

They had blundered down through Piemonte in a mist of road spray until Bert knew he could drive no further. They had taken a slip road, which had got them out of the spray and onto endless country roads. The rain was so heavy and the clouds so low that visibility was non-existent. At the edge of a small town, set among cedar trees and wind-swept poplars, they had found a summer camping-site, now closed, but with its gates left open in silent invitation to autumn tourers.

The river running past the site was high and tawny-coloured. Bert didn't like the look of it, but liked even less the prospect of driving further. He had picked a pitch up on the slope at the edge of the site, well above river level. Then they had splashed up through the town to buy provisions, returning to find another old VW camper was sharing the empty site with them, pitched down near the locked toilet block.

The man had come over in the rain to chat for a bit. A big, quiet German, speaking English that was more precise than Bert could ever manage. As wind and rain gusted through the open door, they had invited him in, a huge, but strangely unthreatening, presence. This was a gentle giant. He had shared their meal with them, going back to his van to bring over a bottle of red wine. His company had filled an empty, stormy night nicely.

Another savage gust sent the van rocking.

'I'm going to turn her round into the wind,' Bert said. 'She will ride out the storm far better that way.'

'In your pyjamas?'

'I won't need to get out,' Bert said. 'We've no mains hook-up. We're wild-camping here. All I need is to slide behind the wheel . . . nobody will see me.'

He climbed out of the warm bed in the rear of the van, pulling on slippers by feel in the dim glow from the fridge light. Pushing into the driving cab, he leaned forward and unclipped the concertina blinds, sliding them back to the edges of the windscreen. Then, slipping into the driving seat, he turned the keys. The engine fired.

Bert switched on the lights, then the wipers. And gaped.

In his headlights, the entire site below him was a lake of slowly moving yellow water. The river had burst its banks. 'Good God,' he exclaimed. 'The whole place is flooded. We're cut off.'

In an instant, Mary was at his side, peering out. 'Are we safe up here?'

'For the minute. But not if it rises any further.'

'Can we get out.'

'Depends how deep it is.' Bert's mind was in emergency mode. There was only one way to find out the depth of the water . . . and he didn't like it. Not one little bit. 'Stay here,' he said. 'I'm going out to see how deep it is, out in the headlights' beam. If we can only make it down to the road through the site, that's still high enough to take us out . . . '

Mary bit her lip. 'Don't do anything crazy. Please.'

He didn't answer, too busy, throwing on a T-shirt, water-proofs and jeans.

'Will I put the lights on inside?' she asked.

'No. I have the headlights.'

'Take care . . . '

She watched him fight to open the side door of the van against the gale. A whirlwind of rain and leaves swept through. Then the door crashed shut, and she waited breath-lessly until his rain-drenched figure appeared in the headlights. As the heavy engine growled, she watched him stagger in the wind. Then he reached the edge of the slowly moving water, hesitated, then waded in purposefully.

Ankle-deep, then shin-deep. Finally, knee-deep.

He disappeared in a squall of rain, then re-emerged, standing on what was obviously the track, with both thumbs up. He must think they could do it. Only then did she realize how fast and loud her heart was beating. She scrambled to get the van ready to move, as he struggled back through the water and the wind. All loose things were simply thrown into their bed and the duvet folded over them. She'd sort it out later, when they were safe.

Another howling blast of wind and rain tore through the van, and the door crashed shut. 'You'd better change,' she said.

'Once we're safe . . . '

He threw himself into the driving seat, soaking everything in rain and river water. She dropped into the passenger seat, as the van lurched away from their pitch and began to head down towards the moving water.

Their headlights swung out across the site, vision cut off and blurred by the density of the rain being driven at them by the gale.

'Oh, Bert,' Mary said faintly. 'The big German's van . . . '

Then they both saw clearly what she had glimpsed. The old VW had yellow water streaming past it, almost halfway up its side. The German had pitched nearer the river, where the flood-water was deeper and the current stronger still.

As Bert hesitated, it seemed as if the VW rocked in his head-lights.

'He must have gone,' he said faintly.

'What if he hasn't?'

As she stared, she heard Bert pull on the handbrake.

'I'm going down,' he said. 'Give him a shout.'

'You could be swept away.' Her voice was high, in panic.

'I won't go in that deep . . . '

'I'm coming with you.'

'You're staying here,' he snapped. 'I need someone in the van. Someone to go for help if it all turns pear-shaped.'

'We can both go for help, right now.'

'No time. Water's rising.'

He left the engine running, and the headlights trained on full beam, pushed past her, lifted the big torch from its cupboard, hesitated, then put it back. The headlights would be strong enough. He might need both hands.

'Take care,' she said, as fresh gales of wind tore through their van.

The door slammed. She watched Bert plough through the ankle-deep water, splashing through shin-deep, ploughing through knee-deep. She saw him stop, probably to shout. Nothing. She saw him hesitate, then move stubbornly deeper, thigh-deep, water surging round his legs in a bow wave. She saw him slip and stagger sideways against its force.

'Bert!' she screamed, alone in the van. This was madness.

All she wanted to do was get out there and drag him back. But, as she rose, she saw him — a tiny figure shrouded in the curtains of driven rain — plough through the water alongside the ancient van. Almost waist-deep now.

He beat on the door with his fist. Then lost patience and dragged the big side door open. The water swept his feet from under him as the door slipped back. Too scared even to scream now, she watched as he hung onto the door, got his feet back under him. He reached forward, taking a grip of something.

Then pulled with all his might.

In her headlights, the VW lurched violently. Then was swept away. But Bert had dragged a huge figure, still wrapped in a sleeping-bag, out on top of him. The two heads bobbed briefly in the headlights. Then were swept off into the dark.

This time there was no stopping her scream. Or her. She was out of the van and into the water, icy cold against her bare feet and legs. The big torch in her hand, she fought to stand upright in a wind that threatened to blow her over, her nightdress acting as a sail.

'BERT!!!!!' she screamed again, searching desperately with the torch beam, beyond the van's headlights. The wind howled round her.

Staggering, she directed the torch beam downstream.

Movement. Something forging through the water. One huge figure with a sack under his arm. Ploughing steadily through the current, a giant struggling against a force that was almost greater than even his strength. The German.

Then the sack hanging beneath his arm writhed, showing a white face as it tried to get free and put its feet down.

'BERT!!!!!' She blundered to meet them, the thigh-deep water catching at her night-dress and leaving her as helpless in the current as a floating branch. She crashed into them, the giant clutching her with his free arm. The torch disappeared, knocked out of her hand and swallowed by the water. Above the storm, she could hear the German gasping from his efforts.

She struggled round, saw Bert's dim face on the other side of the German.

It grinned insanely. 'Told you we should have bought a sat nav,' he said.

As the water grew shallower, the big German eased his grip and let both of them slide feet-first to the ground. 'Your van,' the German gasped. 'Get into it and go fast. Thank you for my life.'

'You're coming, too,' Bert ordered.

'But my van — '

'Could be anywhere between here and Rome.'

'Wrong river.' In the dark, there was a wry smile in the German's voice.

'Whatever.' Bert struggled to open the van door and pushed a sodden Mary through it. The German took over, and bundled him in after her. Then he climbed in himself. It seemed warm, and calm, after the screaming wind outside.

'We go,' the German said. 'And we go fast. Keep your revs high — '

'Or the water might get up the exhaust,' said Bert. 'I know.'

Slipping behind the wheel again, into a sodden driver's seat, Bert eased the van deeper into the floodwater, the engine in first gear to hold the revs high, the sound of water breaking, surging against the moving wheels and underside. The van slithered, swayed, almost lost traction.

'Front-wheel drive?' the German asked. 'Good. I will sit here, on the floor between you. Put my weight over the wheels.'

The van steadied and forged slowly through the flood. A minor bump. Bert sensed the better grip of solid tarmac under the wheels. Turning the van, he steered towards the gap in the wildly waving trees, the exit path to the main road. Leaves streamed across his windscreen and were snatched away again. He grimly kept his foot on the accelerator, ploughing through the flood.

Then there was barely a couple of inches of water. Finally, only muddy puddles and wind-lashed trees in his headlights. He changed up a gear, and the engine settled down to a drone rather than a roar. Within a couple of hundred yards he had reached the road.

'We'd better find the police. Warn them that the river is in flood,' he said.

'The town is built high above the river. It has flooded before, I think,' the German said practically. 'We should just find a place that is safe and dry. Stay there for the night. And see the police in the morning, about my van.'

'Left or right then?' Bert asked.

The massive shoulders shrugged. 'Choose. Trust instinct.'

Bert hesitated, then swung right, away from the town. There had to be a lay-by somewhere, one where they could ride out the storm. But the country road climbed, came to a fork. He hesitated again, then, with a strange sense of certainty, chose the minor road to his right. It climbed steadily, and the town fell behind. No lay-bys here, but up in the shelter of the valley, the wind seemed less.

'There's nowhere to stop,' he muttered.

'*Allahu akbar*,' The German smiled, from the floor. 'God will guide us.'

'That's Arabic,' Mary said.

She waited for an explanation. None came.

'There's a farm ahead,' Bert said, as his headlights swept round a corner, showing an open gateway under swaying cedars. 'We can turn in here. Ask for help. They'll maybe let us stay in their yard until it's day.'

He swung the van through the gates and into a cobbled courtyard. Light spilled from the villa's windows over a line of worksheds. Drawing into a corner, he switched off the engine and his lights. 'We'll be fine here,' he muttered.

Then knew instantly, in his head, that this was so.

'Let's ask them if we can stay,' he said.

'You go,' the German said. 'I will remain here. You did not give me time to dress when you pulled me out of the van and saved my life. I have only pants.'

'I was too busy to notice,' Mary said, pulling her sodden nightdress more tightly round her, and shivering. 'What a nightmare.'

'There is nothing without purpose,' the German said.

'Let's go,' said Bert.

He helped Mary out of the van. The wind was so much easier. The whole place seemed to wrap itself about them offering quiet, and peace. He shook his head: some sort of aftermath from all that adrenalin. A reaction to knowing, when they were both swept away, that they were certain to be drowned. Until the big German had fought free of his sleeping bag, and gathered him up like a child. Rescuing the rescuer. Returning the favour.

Bert knocked quietly on the door. No answer. He knocked again and felt the door open slightly under his hand. He waited, then pushed it open gently. 'Hello,' he called. 'Anyone here?'

Silence. He edged in. An old stone-slabbed kitchen, tall dark furniture, ornately carved. An ancient clock on the wall ticking slowly as if counting out time and centuries in the house. Peace.

At the huge oak kitchen table, there was a small woman sleeping, a half-eaten meal in front of her, a part-empty bottle of wine beside it. Dark-red hair spilled over the folded arms where her head was resting. An empty wine glass stood near the table's edge.

Almost as if sensing she was not alone, an arm jerked suddenly. It caught the glass and sent it spinning across the table. Instinctively,

Bert reached forward and fielded it as it fell. It would have smashed to smithereens on that stone floor.

He looked up to find the woman staring at him, exhausted blue eyes, dark bruises of strain and lack of sleep below them. There were streaks of green and clay across her face. But the eyes were fearless, assessing. First him, then Mary.

'Are you the Old Ones, then?' she asked them quietly. And in English.

★ ★ ★

Kelly looked so much like her mother that it hurt, especially when she was mad at him, as now. David groaned silently. This restaurant treat was part of a belated birthday present. OK, he had planned to nag her about coming back into the routine of study at the university. Instead, he was the one facing the Spanish Inquisition.

'Uh-huh,' he said. Not quite sure what the last in a series of question had been.

'Dad! You weren't listening to a word!'

'Sorry. I was thinking,' he said. 'What were you saying?'

She stared at him, earnest grey eyes in a face the sun never tanned. He heard her take a long, deep breath. 'I asked what your

American research project was,' she ground out. 'And what you were doing about it. And whether or not you had any intention of going there. And when you were going to let go of Mum's memory and move on with your life. Take your pick — but you're answering all of them, before I leave here.'

David grinned. 'I was brought up to respect my elders,' he protested.

'I do. But I'd respect them more, if they answered my questions.'

No escape. 'My research is on the Slave Underground,' he sighed.

'Which is, in words of one syllable?'

'Think American Civil War. Slavery. Slaves running away in the South and trying to reach the freedom offered by the Unionists. In the front-line states, there was a lot of sympathy for slaves. Along the River Ohio, a network of sympathizers risked their lives to smuggle runaways from Kentucky in the South, upriver to Ohio in the North. They called it the Underground Railway.'

Kelly frowned. 'Smuggled them for profit?'

'For religious belief. Arguing that all souls were equal, no matter the colour of skin outside.'

Kelly's frown deepened. 'Surely it's been researched before?'

'Yes. But I'm approaching it through

informal family memories. Oral history, stories passed down through generations — both on the rescuers', and on the slaves' side. Possibly even overlapping — the same stories. Because many of the slaves settled on safe farms near the river. Worked for the small-holders as a concrete way of saying thanks. Then stayed on, as freemen, after the Civil War was over. The socio-culture history scene is big over there. A couple of universities on the river are offering me accommodation and part-time work, to help with the research.'

'Have you written to accept?'

'No. Sabbatical leave was only granted here about ten days ago.'

'Have you any intention of going?'

David shrugged. 'I've still a week to make up my mind.'

'Then go. Don't just strip down someone's car engine, instead.'

'I enjoy mechanic work. It's practical. A break from abstract thinking.'

'Maybe. But it's also become a way of avoiding decisions recently.'

'Ouch!' said David. 'You would get a yellow card for that, in football.'

Kelly studied her father. Outside, he was the same: tall, quiet, humorous and distinguished, hiding the drive and enthusiasm which had kept her family on its toes. It was when you looked into his eyes, or watched his body language, that you saw the differences. The light had gone out of him, the restless body had slipped into neutral. He was drifting. Had lost his way.

'It wasn't your fault, you know,' she said quietly. 'Mum's death.'

'Wrong,' he said bleakly. 'She died because she wrapped the car around a tree. In a temper. Storming out from a blazing row with me, one of many. Caused by my work at the university. She used to say that I lived in a world where dead people and ancient documents were more important than my own family.'

'She knew that wasn't true. Was simply angry, and picking words to hurt.'

'Like we're doing, now?' David asked wryly.

Kelly grinned. 'I thought you would be using the birthday treat to nag me back to work at the university. I was getting my retaliation in first.'

'That's the best way,' David smiled.

She stared at him. 'You should do that more often. Smile. It brings back the dad I knew, not the morose old hermit you've become.'

'More retaliation?'

'Sorry,' she said. 'But if you don't move on, you will destroy your life.'

'You're like a terrier with a stick,' he sighed. 'OK, now that I've suffered your retaliation, when *are* you coming back to take up your Master's studies.'

'I'm not.'

'Then what are you going to do, instead?'

'I'm still thinking about it. Like you.'

'And? What are your thoughts?'

No anger. No outrage at her plans being changed. But her dad had never been like that. His approach was to get you talking — he was such a good listener, he could get a stone to talk. That's why his research work shone: he had the patience to probe, the skill to draw people out, then the mind to fit everything together into a picture so clear you wondered why you'd never seen it yourself. In her uncertainty about the future, Kelly could use some of that right now.

'I enjoyed being my own boss as President of the Students' Union,' she said slowly. 'A thorn in everybody's side. After that, I don't want a dull-as-ditchwater career. Not in big business, anyway — that's all corporate greed, and management's noses in the feeding trough. I want to find something different. Something more . . . acceptable . . . less damaging to either people or our poor polluted planet.'

David waited. As student president, Kelly had led from the front against global warming, against any kind of war, against government policy on single mothers, encroachment of the green belt, whatever. She had fought for every cause that needed a champion. Been bloodied, then come back for more.

'I want to take a year out,' Kelly said. 'Try to do something useful. Add to the world — not simply grab and take away. Maybe in Africa. Maybe South America.'

'You've just had a year out,' he smiled. 'As student president.'

'Now I want another, for myself.' She grinned across the table at him. 'Did I ever embarrass you with my antics? Did the principal ever call you in and tell you to get your daughter under control?'

David's smile broadened. 'A couple of times.'

'And?'

'And I told him that if you didn't care passionately about things like pollution and greed and corruption, then I must have brought you up all wrong.'

'Bless you, Dad,' Kelly said quietly.

David waved over at the waiter for the bill.

'We're both in a mess,' he said. 'We should support each other.'

'Deal,' said Kelly.

David paid the bill, ran her back to her flat, then headed home. An empty place, these days. Four walls, and memories. Not good. Kelly was right: he really must make an effort to get himself back on track again. He owed that to her. He collected the morning mail, then picked up his mobile, which he had left charging.

He flicked through the screen items, checking texts: nothing. Voice mail: one message. He keyed the numbers, waited.

His father's voice. Strained. Frightened.

'David, we need you to come over to Italy immediately. Your mother has collapsed. Been taken into the local hospital. I'm phoning from there. The nearest airport is Turin. There's an evening flight from Edinburgh to Brussels, connecting from there to Turin. If you can make it, text me — my mobile will be off, while I'm inside the hospital. There will be a big German guy called Dieter there, in my van, to collect you.'

A pause, pulsing with worry and uncertainty. 'Please come, David . . . we need you. Can't cope with this on my own. Hurry. Please . . .'

2

One man towered above all other hurrying figures in Turin airport. Almost like a headland, David thought, separate from and standing firmly against the surging tides. Was this the German his father had promised would be there to meet him?

As the flow of travellers carried him closer, David realized it wasn't just sheer size that set the man apart. In the still, set face and remote eyes, there was a sense of withdrawal, even isolation. Someone watching from behind a barrier, used to being alone. Then the blue eyes met his and the brooding face lightened.

'David?' the German asked, stepping forward. 'Are you David Kinsella?'

'You must be Dieter.' They shook hands. David braced himself, but the grip was gentle. 'What's the news of my mother?' he asked.

'She is much better,' Dieter said. 'The doctors are still running tests, but they think it was some form of brainstorm. All her monitor signs are good now — back to normal. They're hopeful that she will recover fully.'

'How did it happen?'

'Out of nowhere. We had been helping Sophie harvest grapes. Your mother went ahead to make dinner. As we came in, she felt dizzy and collapsed. I caught her, and carried her to the room Sophie had given them. She phoned for an ambulance. It took your mother and father straight to hospital. Sophie made me follow in her car — they were old and she was worried about them. But all I did was sit, with your father. When we got your text, he asked me to come and meet you.'

'Thank you.' David's head buzzed with questions. What exactly was a 'brainstorm'? Some sort of seizure, or stroke? If so, would she ever recover fully? How ill was she — and how was he going to handle the crisis, so far from home? He followed the German through the car-park, until they stopped beside a battered, muddy Fiat Punto. 'How long will it take us, to get there?' he asked.

'About one hour thirty. Maybe one hour forty.'

'Let's go,' said David.

★ ★ ★

Mary's collapse put everything into perspective, Sophie thought bleakly. The life of a kindly holidaymaker who had tried to help was more important than getting in the grapes before they softened and were ruined on the vines.

She glanced at the old clock, ticking on the kitchen wall. Its brass pendulum had counted off the triumphs and disasters of many generations, before she and Brian had bought this place on impulse. The slow, heavy tick was soothing. When she was on her own, so hurt and scared she didn't know where to turn, that friendly sound had kept her going. Through its ticking, she sensed the Old Ones watching her. In valley folklore, these were the quiet spirits of the generations who had gone before, clustered around her now as the custodian of their beloved vines. They became her sole companions. She could feel their kindness, their concern, their understanding, because they once had known the same fears and worries.

In her mind, they were so real, that when Bert and Mary had appeared out of nowhere in the night, she honestly believed they were the Old Ones. Instead of ordinary flesh and blood, random strangers drawn into offering help.

Yet they had acted exactly as the Old Ones would have done: simply rolling up their sleeves and making her cause their own. Dieter, the huge German they had brought with them, worked tireless as an ox, carrying the filled crates of grapes up the slopes and into the cellars, freeing her to work full time at cutting, while the other three struggled slowly and painfully to harvest their share.

They had found out that after hours of reaching down into the vines, your back is ready to snap in two, while the hand that holds the cutters is soon weeping with broken blisters. She had seen Bert switch the cutter to his left hand and known the reason why. As for Dieter, there had been blood from his hands on the edges of the crates. Her own hands were calloused, toughened, by now. Not theirs. Yet they had worked uncomplainingly.

Now Mary was in hospital.

Sophie buried her face in her hands. Red hair spilled over the work-reddened knuckles with their scars and scratches. If only someone would phone and let her know how Mary was . . .

Her head snapped up. Outside, the sound of car tyres in the yard. A squeal of brakes that needed replacing, in a car that only held together out of habit. She jumped from her chair at the kitchen table and ran to the door. Throwing it open, she looked out to the soft purple darkness of the Piemonte autumn night.

Into the light cast by the doorway, came two figures. Dieter's huge frame and another stranger who would be tall in anyone else's company. Dark hair fell over a sombre, intelligent face.

'Have you any news?' she cried. 'How is Mary?'

'Fine. Sleeping now — with my dad probably sleeping in the chair beside her bed.' The man stopped, in the doorway. 'I am David,' he said. 'Mary's son. You must be Sophie. Dieter has been talking about you all night long.'

'You got him talking?' she asked, surprised.

Dieter shrugged. 'This quiet man could get a stone to talk.'

'What happened to your mother? Do they know?' Sophie asked.

'It was a transient ischaemic attack — a sort of mini-stroke,' David said. 'The blood vessels seize up and starve the brain of blood. People collapse, lose the power of their legs and tongue. Then the blood starts flowing again and the symptoms usually disappear.' He sighed. 'It can happen to an older person at any time, for no particular reason. It may be the first of several attacks, or a one-and-only. There is no treatment. No way of knowing if it will happen again. She can only rest for a couple of days, then pick up her life.'

'Poor Mary,' said Sophie. 'It's all my fault.'

'*Insha Allah*,' Dieter said quietly. 'It is God's will. And nobody's fault.'

David glanced across sharply. 'Dieter's right,' he said. 'These things happen. I'm just grateful it happened here when the two of you could take over. If they had been away on their own, in that campervan of theirs . . . '

'They would have coped,' Dieter said. 'Your father saved my life in a raging flood. He is a strong man. In a crisis, he will always find survival skills.'

'Maybe so,' said David. 'I'm still grateful that you got them quickly into the hospital.' Wearily, he rubbed his eyes. It had been a very long and stressful day.

'Can I get you something to eat? Coffee? Tea?'

'A mug of coffee would be good,' said David.

As Sophie passed him, Dieter touched her wrist. 'David thinks he might be able to get your tractor working,' he said quietly.

Sophie spun round. 'Can you really? It would make a huge difference to the amount of grapes we could harvest. We're wasting too much time carrying the full crates manually up the slopes to the cellars.'

'Dieter admitted he had his own reason for wanting your tractor working.'

Dieter grimaced. 'One day of being the

tractor is enough for any man.' He beamed at Sophie. 'Yet Sophie was cutting grapes and carrying crates by herself for days before we came. This is no ordinary woman.'

Sophie felt herself blushing. Silly. 'A working tractor would transform our chances.'

'I'll do my best,' David promised. 'Working with mechanical things — it's the one useful skill I have. According to my daughter, most academics have no useful skills at all.'

Sophie found herself smiling. It was a long time since her last smile. 'I'll get the coffee,' she said. 'While you're drinking it, I'll get a room ready for you. You can have a look at the tractor in the morning.'

'I'd rather take it to bits and start working on it now.'

'But it's almost three a.m.'

'And you will be harvesting grapes, in three hours' time.'

'I'm not being heartless,' Sophie said. 'But if Mary's safe, then I must try to get more of the harvest in. I have today, and maybe one further day before they spoil. Without the grapes, there is no wine. Without wine to sell, I am bankrupt.'

'Dieter told me. If I have the tractor ready, then I can help you cut the grapes as well. Three sets of hands are better than two.'

Sophie swallowed: after months of isolation

41

it was difficult not to be emotional when total strangers gave her what she needed most — direct help, not just words of sympathy. 'Thanks,' she said, inadequately.

As they left, she busied herself around the kitchen. Yes, she would be out harvesting again as soon as there was light. No matter how impossible the task, she wasn't giving in. Least of all now, when she had help. She wasn't on her own any more. For the very first time, she found herself daring to hope.

★ ★ ★

Cramped into the shape of the hospital chair, Bert was suddenly very much awake.

He scrubbed gritty eyes. Mary was on the edge of the bed, in the faded floral nightgown the hospital had given her. Inside its folds she seemed small and lost.

'What do you think you're doing?' he demanded, trying to guide her back.

Weakly, she pushed his hands away. 'Not yet,' she said. 'Let me sit until my head clears.' Her words were slightly slurred.

Above them, on the wall of the side-ward they had been given, the electric clock ticked and its hand jumped forward half a minute. Outside, muted noises from the ward and foreign voices. Scary.

'How do you feel?' Bert asked. 'Will I fetch a nurse?'

Mary's mouth twitched into a lop-sided smile. 'No. Save your one word of Italian for another time,' she said. 'I'm just muddled. I've got to concentrate before I try to move. Don't think I can stand up yet.'

'Then don't. I'll get the nurse.'

'Don't need a nurse.' Slowly, she turned to him. 'What happened to me, Bert? I don't remember anything. Yes, I do. I remember getting the meal ready. I remember you all coming in. Then everything went blurred . . . '

'You took a funny turn,' he said gently.

'Didn't make me laugh.'

'Nor us. You . . . sort of fainted.'

Mary's face came up. It might have been imagination, but there seemed a lot more life in it. No longer the slack, old woman's face that had scared him rigid.

'Bert,' she said, 'I'm not your mother. You're not trying to find a diplomatic way of telling me that you've been keeping moth caterpillars in the wardrobe. This is me, Mary. So stop messing about. What happened? What's wrong with me?'

Bert hesitated. 'You had some sort of temporary brain seizure,' he said.

'OK. It's good to know I have a brain. What do you mean by seizure?'

'A mild sort of shock,' he said. 'They're pretty sure it isn't permanent. The doctor will explain things better.'

'Maybe. But I'd rather hear it from you first. What exactly happened?'

'Something cut off the blood supply to your brain. You blacked out. Now everything's working OK again. They said you'd get your speech back first. Then your movement. And that there won't be any lasting damage.'

He found himself repeating the last words silently. Like a prayer.

Mary was watching closely. 'No lasting damage?'

'Cross my heart,' Bert said.

'It's on the other side,' she told him. But I'll be OK?'

'They said you'll be back to your nagging best, by tomorrow.'

'Don't they know I've got to do your thinking for you? Pull all your strings?'

'I didn't tell them.'

Mary smiled. Bert's heart leapt when he saw it was a proper smile, not one with bits of it dragging. And her eyes were clear. Somebody was living in there again. Maybe they were right; her recovery would be quick and complete.

'Will I get you a cup of tea?' he asked.

'Just a minute.' Now that the fuzzy edges were sharpening, Mary's brain kicked in. This was a wake-up call, finishing up in a foreign hospital like this. Right now, her brave words about following the wind like a gypsy seemed hollow. Go on, or go back? She needed to talk this over with somebody she could trust. Someone on the same wavelength.

'We should phone Kelly,' she said.

'No need. David's here.'

She stared at him. 'He's in America.'

'No. He's at Sophie's place. He changed his plans. Came here.'

Mary's eyes filled. That was good — and bad. Good that he had dropped everything to come over and help them sort out the mess. Bad, because he was likely to overreact, and pull the plug on their great adventure before it had scarcely begun. Maybe it was over, but her instinct was to protect their independence.

Bert watched her massage her brow. 'Will I fetch a doctor?' he asked.

'Don't need a doctor. Just take me home.'

'We have no home . . . ' he said helplessly.

'Yes, I know,' she said impatiently. 'We sold the house and bought the campervan. *That's* our home now. That's where I want to be. Not in that woman's place. Not here.' She glanced around. 'I can't stand hospitals. They scare me.'

'Just as well that something does,' he said.

Mary looked surprised, then began to laugh. 'Bert,' she said, 'you've been acting like an undertaker. Have you finally decided that I'm going to live?'

'I'm going for that cup of tea,' he said stolidly, heading for the door.

'Bert!'

'What?' He paused in the doorway.

'Can you make it a proper breakfast?' she asked. 'I'm starving.'

★ ★ ★

As daylight grew, Kelly turned over in bed. No good: she would never get back to sleep. Her mind was full of what her father had told her over his mobile, while he was rushing for Edinburgh Airport.

How could this happen when her gran was so far from home? Kelly struggled to the edge of her bed, glancing at her watch. Barely 6 a.m. — did that mean 7 a.m. or 8 a.m. over there? Was it still too early to phone her father?

Padding barefoot over to the window of her flat, Kelly peeped through the curtains. A cold grey dawn without so much as a stray cat slipping along the pavements of Dundee. She loved the place, but she wanted away from it — only she didn't know where to go, or what to do. Did that make any sense?

You can't run from your problems, her father had told her. They're in your head and in your heart and you'll only take them with you. She knew he was speaking from experience — her mother's death and his omnipresent sense of loss and guilt. If he didn't find closure, move on, he would destroy himself.

Kelly crossed the dark hallway and tapped on her flatmate's door.

No answer. She knocked again, more loudly. Silence. Opening the door, she walked over to her friend's bed and gently shook the mound under the duvet.

'Debbie! Debbie! Are you awake?'

A startled grunt. 'What's happened? Is the house on fire?'

'I need to talk something through.'

'Mmphm.' Debbie slid peacefully towards the escape of sleep.

'Debbie! It's urgent!'

'I'm listening.'

'You're not. You're half asleep.'

A resigned sigh, followed by a weak struggle, as Debbie levered herself into a sitting position. Eyes tight shut, she asked, 'Whazza time?'

'About six.'

'In the *morning*?' One baleful eye opened. 'I only got back from working, four hours ago . . . '

'You've all day to sleep.'

'I have a class at ten.' Debbie tried to yawn, but it took too much energy. 'OK. What's the problem?'

'My gran's been taken into hospital. Somewhere near a little village, called Alba, up in the wine country of Piemonte.'

'And?'

'And I think I should go over there. Help them out.'

'Then go.' Debbie slid gently into a more horizontal position.

'You're my friend. You're supposed to be arguing me out of it!'

'Then don't go. G'night.'

'Debbie!'

'Huh?'

'My dad's gone over. He'll get mad if I turn up too. But I want to be with them. I know what they're like . . . I speak their language. I'm probably closer to them than he is. They're not just grandparents, they're my friends. Partners in crime, when they should have been setting me a good example.

48

We're three of a kind. I should be over there right now, helping them to pick up the pieces. Staying on for a bit, to make sure they're all right. He'll just bring them home.'

'Maybe that's where they should be?'

'No. They don't realize they're old yet. They're as young inside as me. If Dad brings them back, he's taking away the magic spark that keeps them going. It could destroy them, make them old, dependent, overnight.'

'Maybe they *are* dependent?'

'Anything but. They've gone off to tour the world on their own in their motorhome. Wintering where it stays warm, then following the spring north.'

'Excellent. Well, the answer's obvious.'

'What?'

'Get a good breakfast inside you. Hit the road. I'll wash your dishes.'

'Debbie, you're a star.'

'I'm a star who's a stone overweight.'

'That only makes you a bigger star,' Kelly smiled.

'G'way. Let me catch up on sleep. Send me a postcard, girl.'

'You've got it.'

Kelly hurtled round the house, breakfasting and packing on the run. She threw a handful of everything into an old travel bag that had followed her through thick and thin. How was her granddad coping? She feared the worst. He needed Gran, to tell him what to do. But she was sick now. Maybe dying.

Kelly couldn't let her die. Together they were the Three Musketeers, facing anything that life could throw at them, shoulder to shoulder. That's where she should be now, standing beside them. That was her place. Her duty.

Grabbing her mobile, she scrolled to her father's number, then pressed. Long wait. Then the automated voice: *sorry . . . this number is not available*. That meant his mobile was switched on, but was out of signal. Where? Just when she needed to speak to him urgently.

Pointlessly, she dialled again. Same reply. No time to wait.

She was going. Act first, argue later.

Kelly checked her watch. Hours before the bank would open, but there was always the hole-in-the-wall machine. And her credit card. First, she must catch a train to Edinburgh. Then the airport bus. Once there, find out which flight to take — anything to a European hub with a link to Turin. Then, somehow, get a ticket. After that, she would make up the day as she went along.

With one last look round her shared flat, she was off through the door, her feet skimming down the winding stairs. The front door to the communal entrance of the flats creaked once, twice. Then banged shut. Leaving nobody but the seagulls overhead to listen to her running feet.

★   ★   ★

It was almost dawn when David finished work on the small tractor. He straightened wearily, wiping black oil and grease off his hands onto a rag.

This was like no tractor he had seen before. A tiny, ancient Fiat, sitting low on caterpillar tracks, designed for working on steep slopes and between the tight lines of vine trellises. Its time-worn diesel engine had needed stripping, cleaning, its filters solid with filth, beyond rescue. He had fitted an old set of spares, found in a crumbling cardboard box. Would they work?

Wiping his hands, he went to the work bench where he'd left his wrist watch for safety. Still set at British time — and his brain was too tired to make the simple conversion. But it was too early to start the tractor and wake everybody. Cold diesel engines, particularly work-worn ones, sounded as if they were falling apart, until they warmed up and the parts expanded to fit tight together.

He pushed open the workshed door and looked out to a crisp, almost purple pre-dawn. The scent of cedars filled his nostrils. The villa — with no lights showing — was a dark outline against the sky. A deep silence hung over everything.

Gradually, he became conscious of a muffled scrubbing noise. Then saw light spilling through an outhouse door. Savouring the tang of cedars and faint woodsmoke, he wandered over, hesitated outside the part-open door, then entered.

At first, the cellar lights dazzled him. The outhouse was bigger than he'd realized, with tall gleaming metal vats along either side. Against one of these, high on a ladder, the red-haired woman was scrubbing vigorously down the inside of the tank with a long-handled brush.

It was warm in the cellar: he closed the door.

'Leave it open. It's venting fermentation gases.' Sophie wiped sweat from her face. 'One of them is dangerous — and doesn't smell. In the old days, people kept a dog with them while they worked. If it fell over, they got out. Fast.'

'Like miners took canaries down the pits,' said David. 'What are you doing?'

'Getting a couple of vats ready for today's

pressing. Can you pass up that hose, until I flush this out?'

David reached up, then steadied the ladder as she worked with frowning concentration. 'How many vats are fermenting?' he asked.

'Three. It should be ten.'

'How many days' work in each vat?'

She flicked a stray strand of hair off her face. 'On my own, it took three days to cut enough grapes to press and fill the first. We did the other two yesterday, with Dieter carrying the crates, freeing me to work full time. Your parents helped.' She paused. 'I'm truly sorry about your mother.'

'The doctor said it could have happened anywhere.'

'I still feel guilty. Turn off the water, please.'

Wearily, Sophie came down the ladder with the hose.

'Have you been to bed?' he asked.

'Have you?'

'I wanted to get your tractor working.'

'And did you?'

'I think so. Haven't fired the engine yet — it would waken the neighbourhood.'

She smiled tiredly. 'Not at harvest time. That's when the valley people go round each vineyard in turn, as a volunteer army. Most of them will be up already and out on somebody's slopes as soon as it's light enough.'

'Why not your slopes?'

'Our fault — or Brian's anyway. My ex-husband — he's working in financial services again, back in London. We came over here to reinvent ourselves and rescue a marriage that was heading for the rocks.'

She fell silent: so difficult to rake over old ashes, but she wanted to talk the issues through with somebody who might understand. 'At first, the valley people welcomed us. They judge you by how hard you work, and Sergio — one of their leaders — once said to me: 'you work like a man', which was the biggest compliment he could pay me. The whole culture of the valley is about helping one another. They think nothing of dropping in when they're passing, and working alongside you for an hour or so at whatever chore you're doing. Just as you would chat to a friendly neighbour, over a gate, back home. They were my friends . . . '

'And?' he prompted, when her voice faltered.

'There's two sides to any problem,' she said finally. 'They didn't like Brian because he never worked on the slopes. He handled the business side of things — he was into planning and marketing. But he thought they were primitives, too. He started reading books on growing grapes and making wine, and it was all high tech against their common-sense advice. He began behaving like a know-it-all, telling the locals their business when they'd only come to help. So they walked out on him, and on me. Over here, it's assumed that the woman will always back her man. I was on their side. Instead of curing all our problems, our new venture brought them to a head. Our marriage fell apart. I got the vineyard in our divorce settlement and inherited the people problems Brian left behind.'

In the open doorway of the cellar, they stood companionably, watching the horizon turn red. 'Dieter's right,' she said. 'You could get a stone to talk.'

'It's my job,' said David.

'What about tractors?'

'Mending cars has always been a hobby.'

She stood beside him, watching his reactions as the sky glowed orange and the first rays of sunlight spilled over the softly-rolling hills of the Langhe, turning the mist in their broad valleys into a sea of molten gold.

'It's so beautiful here,' he said.

'I thought so, too,' said Sophie. 'I staked my family's future on it . . .'

Her voice broke. He waited patiently, as the sun climbed higher.

'And I lost,' she added, so quietly he barely heard. 'I have two girls. One thirteen, the other fifteen, over in a boarding-school in England. Our break-up has scarred them both. Now, this financial mess. I'm terrified I'll lose them. Then I will have absolutely nothing. No husband. No family. And no vineyard.'

He glanced down. The rising sun turned the streak left by a tear into a tiny rivulet of gold. He wanted to reach out and wipe it away. He pushed his dirty hands further into his pockets.

Sophie sensed in him a quiet strength that was like water running deep, and she sensed compassion. He understood: without judgement or condemnation. In the early dawn, she felt comfortable in this man's company.

'It's like a chain,' David finally said. 'Mend one link, then move to the next one, then the next. You haven't lost the vineyard yet. Let's start that tractor. If it's working, then Dieter and I will help you make the best shot of harvesting your grapes that the three of us can manage.'

'If I can even fill six vats — ' she started.

'One link at a time,' David chided. 'Let's give that tractor its chance.'

56

The old Fiat started with a cough and a splutter. David busied himself with a spanner and tried again. This time, it burst into a healthy roar. He glanced up, smiling, oil streaks across his face. 'Like Chairman Mao said, the longest journey starts with but a single step.'

His smile was infectious.

'Can you hold your Long March until I fetch my jacket?' Sophie asked.

★　★　★

'Dieter doesn't say much,' Sophie commented. Her hands flew along the vines, cutting and laying the cones of purple grapes into the plastic crate at her feet.

'Too busy working.' David straightened wearily. He'd forgotten when he last had sleep, his back ached, his hands were blistered from the cutters and his face and arms were almost as filthy from green chemicals, as Sophie's.

'He works,' she agreed. 'I could use another fifty like him. And you.'

'We're too slow,' said David. 'Amateurs.'

'This is my third harvest. You maybe think I'm fast, but you should see the valley people who have been harvesting all their lives.'

In the golden heat of mid-afternoon, they

worked easily together.

'He's *always* quiet,' Sophie said, like a terrier whose teeth have closed on a stick, and can't let go. 'Just a big gentle presence. A listener. Somebody who adds the odd word, here and there.'

She dragged her crate forward. 'Then there are these Arabic words he comes up with. Usually some quote about God, or Allah. But, as soon as he's spoken, he clams up, and you realize that it was a private thought. Like he was talking to himself, and you weren't meant to hear. Was he like that in the car?'

David switched the secateurs to his other hand. 'Not really,' he said.

'What did he talk about?'

'Mainly you. You've made a big impression.'

'I don't know why. I'm so tired and dirty. Bad-tempered.'

David smiled. 'Maybe he sees beneath the dirt to the woman underneath.'

Sophie laughed. 'What if she's tired and dirty and bad-tempered too?'

'Aren't we all?' he said.

He straightened slowly. Soon, they would have filled enough crates to make another load for the tractor. His job. He glanced up to the top of the slope, to see a darkly dressed old woman watching them. 'We've got company,' he said.

Sophie turned. 'It's Maria,' she said, surprised. 'She used to keep the house for me. What can she want? Not a message from the hospital, surely?'

'My dad would have phoned me direct,' said David.

Sophie locked her secateurs, and stuffed them into a pocket of her grape-stained jeans. 'Better go up and see,' she decided.

David wiped sweat from his face and caught Dieter grinning.

'You looked better, green,' the German said.

'What *is* the stuff?' asked David.

'It's sprayed on the leaves in early summer, to stop insect infestation. How is your back? Your hands?'

'I'm wrecked,' said David. 'But Sophie just goes on . . . '

Dieter studied his own damaged hands. 'What we have cut this morning will barely fill another vat,' he said. He flexed his fingers, wincing. 'What she needs is unattainable. By midday tomorrow, she thinks the grapes will be too oily for good wine. We are like three ants, trying to do the work of a colony.'

'Absolutely. We need more hands — a whole village of people. That's why they go round each other's vineyards, helping.'

Dieter began to clip again. 'Perhaps so. But she has only us.'

At the top of the slope, Sophie reached Maria. The older woman held out a small wicker basket, covered with a bright clean teacloth.

'I heard your tractor leave this morning. Saw you working with these two men when we passed to help at Sergio's. I've brought some sandwiches — and three bottles of my sons' beer.'

'Won't they complain?' asked Sophie.

Maria snorted. 'They will complain, but I will not listen. I am their mother, who once changed their diapers. Wiped their noses. Scolded them, when they were naughty. Why should I fear them now?'

'*Grazie*,' Sophie said, taking the basket.

'*Prego*. You work too hard. You do not rest. You do not eat. What would your own mother say? Who are these men? Are they hired men, from the town?'

'They are strangers.'

'Then why are they helping you? For cash?'

'I have no money. They are helping because there is no one else to help.'

A tear gathered in Maria's eye. Impatiently, she scrubbed it away. 'I know what your mother would have said. She would have asked you: have you another pair of cutters,

60

and I will help you too.'

'You are not my mother.'

'I would have been proud to have so strong a daughter. Instead, I have been shamed by strangers. Men who came from nowhere. As if by magic, because no one else was there to offer help, when it was so clearly and so badly needed. The Old Ones must have sent them. Give me a set of cutters, and I will help you too . . . '

Sophie embraced the older woman. 'Thank you from my heart,' she said, in the French/Italian *patois* of the valleys. 'But, Maria, what good are two more willing hands? The grapes are growing soft on me already. I am ruined.'

'Then we are all ruined,' Maria said, pushing herself away. 'You, because your slopes are full of grapes going soft, and the valley because our hearts are full of guilt. But were too proud, have taken far too long, to soften.'

She turned back to the cart track and began to trudge away.

'Go with God,' called Sophie after her.

3

Even the darkness felt strange and foreign. David gave up trying to sleep and swung his legs over the edge of the bed. There was a faint glow of light through the curtains. He padded over, looking out to a world of uncertain shapes and soft shadows in the courtyard below Sophie's villa. He craned his head: the sky to his right was lightening. Dawn was coming.

David and sleep had been strangers since his wife's accident. He paused, considering: by the time he washed his face, and climbed into his filthy grape-stained shirt and jeans from yesterday, there would be light enough to see outside. If he could see, then he could cut grapes. Better than hanging about with only his thoughts for company. But he must leave quietly. There was still a world where normal people slept. He envied them.

Ten minutes later, he eased out through the kitchen door, and tiptoed across the court-yard. No wonder everything had seemed fuzzy: a cold grey mist lay thick across the valley, wrapping itself like a familiar cat around him. He shivered.

Collecting secateurs from the workshed, he headed along the track to the slopes where they'd been working yesterday. Today, vision within the swirling mist was less than twenty yards, creating a different world, where only the deep silence of the valley was familiar.

He slithered down the slope, carrying a couple of plastic crates for the grapes he would cut. The rows of misty vines on either side looked identical. Without landmarks, he felt disorientated. Where had they finished the night before?

Fragments of dried clay pattered down the slope behind him. Dieter? He waited, but a smaller figure emerged from the mist. 'Sophie?' he asked.

'I heard you get up and go out. Guessed what you were doing. I was on the point of starting early myself. So I threw on some clothes and came out after you.'

'What about Dieter?'

'Still sleeping.' White teeth flashed in the mist. 'Snoring his head off.'

'I can't remember where we stopped. Everything looks different in the mist.'

'It's further down. We get a lot of mist in the wine valleys. Something to do with the big Alps over to the west, with snow on them already. And the warm water of the Gulf of Genoa below us.' Sophie pulled a face. 'I was never much good at geography, but cold air meeting warmer air, makes mist.'

'What big Alps to the west?'

'In the far distance, the French side. Most days, you never see them. But if the air's scrubbed clear because a big storm's coming, or it's frosty everywhere, then a whole range of huge mountains jumps out at you. Alpine skiing country.'

Droplets of water beaded on her red hair. The mist became golden, as the sun climbed over the Langhe's hills. In that soft light, she looked as if she had stepped from a Renaissance painting.

'I'll take your word for it,' David said.

'Here's where we start. But let me check the grapes first.'

He watched her feel half a dozen purple cones of fruit. She looked up, uncertainly. 'I simply don't know — I'm not expert enough. These are softer than any grapes I've cut before. But this is only my third harvest.' She reached for another cone of grapes, biting her lip.

'What happens if they are too soft?' he asked.

'The fruit goes oily. And that passes, through the pressing, into the wine.'

'Could it ruin what we have harvested earlier?'

'No. Those grapes are already pressed, and the wine is fermenting. We can only ruin what we do today, if I guess wrong, and we cut some more.'

'Then it sounds like a risk you can take.'

Sophie had the feeling that he was gently nudging her forward, simplifying the decision that she had to make. 'I need every vat of drinkable wine we can get,' she said quietly. 'If the grapes feel too soft, just leave them and move to another bunch — it takes too long to prune out the soft ones.'

'Then let's get on with it,' David said.

The handles of the cutters hurt his blistered hands. He winced, then carried on stoically. As his father Bert was prone to say, it was likely to get worse, before it got better. He wondered how his mother was.

Above them from the passage down the slope, came the sound of someone slithering, then an almighty crash. Whoever it was, had come a cropper. But there was no cry of pain. No explosion of cursing. Silence. Then a patter of clay flakes came down the slope, as the person started down again.

'That can only be Dieter,' David said.

The huge figure loomed out of the mist. 'You left me behind,' it complained.

'We thought you needed your beauty sleep,' smiled David.

'It would take more than sleep to make me beautiful,' Dieter said. 'Where do you want me to start, Sophie?'

'Take the row below me.'

'Why not the row above you, where I can watch, and learn?'

'That's claimed already,' David said. 'It's mine. Go away.'

'No. You cheated, and came out early. Let's toss a coin for it.'

Dieter's eyes were twinkling. Sophie sensed the banter was staged, to cheer her up, reduce the tension.

'Be quiet,' said Sophie. 'You are worse than children, both of you.'

'Yes, ma'am,' they said together.

'Stop it,' she laughed. 'You make me feel like a school-teacher.'

As the mist turned into a torrent of gold which flowed around them on the slopes of the valley, they worked companionably. Sophie the fastest: Dieter, his hands now toughening up, gradually finding a rhythm; while David, the blisters on his hands already weeping, worked on doggedly. The only sound in the valley, the click of their cutters, and the scrape as someone dragged their plastic crate along a yard or too. Then, as the world awoke, came the sound of wood pigeons, the harsh cry of magpies, and the distant barking of a dog.

Schoolteacher, indeed. How were her two girls getting on at their school in England? Had Brian kept his promise and paid their term fees? Everything was such a mess. Impossible. Sandwiched between her two helpers, Sophie flew at the grapes. Today, probably only this morning, was the last chance she would ever have of making enough from her harvest to meet the interest payments on the vineyard, letting her keep her dream, hang on desperately to the debt-burdened home, which she had bought to pass down to her daughters.

She paused, wiping sweat from her eyes. Strange, the house she had bought for her own family was filling up with someone else's family. Strangers, brought here by a force she didn't understand. She knew nothing of them; they knew nothing of her. Yet they had made her problem theirs, and she had accepted their help, as if it was the most natural thing on earth.

She was no longer on her own. The easy company of the two men working beside her on the slopes had brought her new belief, determination. Her shoulders squared. Sophie didn't do defeat. She would fight on until she had nothing left to give. For her dream of the future. For the vineyard that she loved, and her girls whom she loved even more. There were only hours left to save what she could from her harvest.

No time for self pity — or self doubt.

★ ★ ★

The Italian cab blasted around a tight bend in the valley road. Tyres whined, then screamed. The driver nonchalantly held the wheel with one hand, his mobile phone in the other. The rear end broke away, fish-tailed, came back under control, then the turbo howled as the driver floored his accelerator.

In the back seat, Bert disentangled himself from Mary. 'I could have done with this driver forty years ago,' he gasped.

'Forty years ago, that would have got your face slapped,' said Mary. She grabbed at Bert, as the next bend in the hill road flew towards them. The driver changed his mobile casually to his other hand. More screaming tyres. 'Whose idea was this?' she demanded.

'Yours.'

'Then it was a good idea,' she said firmly, holding onto him grimly.

'You wanted to get out of that hospital as soon as daylight broke.'

'Given the chance, I'd have left in the middle of the night.'

'We should have phoned Sophie's,' Bert muttered. 'Got David or Dieter to come and collect us.'

Trellises of vines streaked past the side windows. The nearside wheels left the tarmac road, sliding onto the hard-baked chalk clay. The speeding taxi bounced, clouds of white dust blooming out behind. Then bumped back onto tarmac.

Mary opened her eyes. 'They're too busy getting in the harvest. We can get there on our own . . . do all Italians drive like this?'

'Probably.'

She wedged herself more firmly into the seat. 'We can't have people running after us, not while we're able to look after ourselves.'

Bert stared at her. 'Look after ourselves?' he demanded 'You've just spent forty-eight hours in emergency, tubes dangling out of you like spaghetti — '

'Too much information.'

'You're an invalid. We should have asked for help to get home. Not just signed you out of the place. You were safer in that hospital . . . '

'Look, they said that all I needed was a couple of days' rest. I've been in bed since Tuesday. What's your problem?'

Bert clutched his head. 'You'll be the death of me,' he complained.

69

'Waste of time. You're too old to get insurance cover.'

He took a firmer grip round her waist as the next bend loomed. The taxi driver was in mid-argument on his phone, one finger wagging angrily in front of his face — from the hand that should have been holding the wheel.

At the last possible moment, a casual reach forward sent them hurtling around the bend. Bert and Mary slid across the back seat, seat belts biting deep. As the car steadied, out of the hill mist on the road ahead Bert saw someone: a young woman, carrying an old travel bag, which seemed familiar.

They flashed past the plodding figure.

Bert tapped urgently on the driver's shoulder. '*Arretez*,' he shouted.

'That's French,' said Mary. 'Well, nearly French.'

'I'm sure that was Kelly,' Bert said. He struggled to turn and look back as the car sawed madly to a halt. The young woman disappeared into the mist and clay dust. 'Stay!' he shouted at the driver, opening the door. A stream of angry Italian followed him. He ignored it completely, and ran back down the road.

He found her coughing, wiping chalk dust from her eyes.

'What in the name o' the wee wally dug, are you doing here?' he demanded.

Kelly sneezed. 'I've come to rescue you,' she said.

'We nearly ran you down.'

'Who cares. I've found you.' Kelly hugged her grandfather fiercely. She smelled of long journeys in hot spaces, and looked exhausted. 'Where's Gran? Is she still in hospital?' she asked.

'They've still to build the hospital that would hold her,' Bert lamented.

Kelly grinned. 'I could have told you that. Is she up in the car?'

'Unless she's run on ahead. She's in escape mode.'

Kelly picked up her travel bag. 'How is she? What happened? Nobody phoned to tell me what's going on.'

'She's fine,' said Bert. 'But she gave us a scare. A temporary black-out.'

They reached the car and Mary dragged Kelly inside. Bert and the travel bag had nowhere left to go but the seat beside the driver. Bert thought longingly of the relative safety of the back. 'OK. Go!' he said, pointing ahead.

The car leapt forward.

'How did you know where we were?' Mary asked, holding Kelly's hand tight.

'Dad gave me the vineyard's address. When I got to Alba, I went into the *carabinieri*. I showed them the address and they drew me a map. I'd run out of money, and it was nearly daylight by then, so I walked.'

'How on earth did you get to Alba?' Mary demanded.

'Oh, trains and planes and buses. You name it. I've been on the road non-stop since yesterday morning. Or was it the day before?'

'But why?'

'You were in hospital. I wanted to be there with you and Granddad.'

Mary swallowed, but the tears still came. 'Bless you, Kelly,' she said.

'Where is this woman's vineyard?' asked Kelly.

'Near the head of the valley,' Bert shouted back.

They all went silent as the car screamed around another tight bend.

'It was better walking,' gasped Kelly.

'You get used to it, after a bit,' said Mary. 'He hasn't hit anything, yet.'

The taxi turned on two wheels through a stone gateway, into a courtyard under ancient cypress trees. They climbed out shakily. Bert fumbled in his wallet for the few euros he had left. The driver's hand flicked in, and picked the biggest of the notes. '*Ciao*,' he said. Then the taxi roared away.

In the thinning mist, Kelly admired the warm colours of the old villa, and the pantiles of its outhouses around the cobbled courtyard. After the noise of the taxi, everything was quiet. Expectant, almost, as if the house itself was watching them, but welcoming too. Strange notion. She inhaled the scent of the cypresses. Above her head, wood pigeons crooned. Beyond the villa, she could see in soft focus the endless geometric lines of vines covering every inch of ground.

'What a gorgeous place,' she said. 'Where do we go?'

'The van?' asked Mary, looking longingly to where that was parked in the far corner of the courtyard.

'Don't even think of it,' Bert said, clutching Kelly's travel case. 'You're confined to barracks for a few days yet.'

'You're going to have to speak to him, Kelly,' Mary complained.

'About what?' Kelly was still admiring her surroundings.

'The man's treating me like an invalid.'

'You are an invalid.'

Mary hauled her round. 'Look, did you come all this way to take *his* side?'

Kelly sighed. 'I came to be on both your sides.'

'Not good enough. It's *my* side you should be on. I've been poorly.'

'Condemned by your own evidence, Gran,' said Kelly. 'The house it is, for you . . . ' Her voice faltered. 'But maybe I could borrow your van for a bit, and crash down in it. I can't just dump myself on the woman, can I? What am I going to say?'

Until that moment, getting there had been her sole priority. Now that she had collected her two charges, she was too tired to think about what came next.

'Don't worry. Sophie's nice,' said Bert. He beat off Kelly's weary grab to reclaim her bag, and trudged towards the kitchen. Pushing the door open, he stepped inside. 'Hello, the house!' he called.

They crowded in behind him. A cool, tall farmhouse kitchen, full of ornate old-fashioned furniture. A huge dark-oak kitchen table, set out with three breakfast places. There was an almost tangible sense of peace through the old house.

'Looks like they're expecting us,' said Mary. 'But how did they know?'

Above them, on the wall, an old brass pendulum swung. The heavy tick of the clock seemed to echo not just through the house, but through many years of time.

'Where is everybody?' asked Mary.

'It's like the *Marie Celeste*,' whispered Kelly.

★ ★ ★

The dawn mist was thinning, as the Piemonte sun grew stronger. The floor of the valley was still hidden, but now only tendrils of mist drifted between the vines. David straightened painfully.

His stomach grumbled.

'I heard that,' Dieter said.

Sophie massaged her back. 'I left the table set for us,' she said. 'Maybe we should go back up and have some breakfast?'

'There's no time to eat,' said Dieter. 'We can catch up later.'

'Are you sure?' asked Sophie.

'Sure he's sure,' said David.

Sophie anxiously felt the grapes. 'It's probably only my imagination,' she muttered. 'But they seem softer every time.'

'Let's cut until midday, then decide what to do,' said David.

'We'll never cut enough,' mourned Dieter. 'If only I'd come here days ago.'

'I had to flood a river to bring you here,' said Sophie.

'And destroy my van.' Dieter smiled wryly back at her. 'These Old Ones of yours — did they have to play so rough, when they were recruiting us?'

'Were you insured?' asked David.

'It was a very old van. Only insured for the damage it did. From what the police say, the flood swept it down the valley for two kilometres. It is full of mud. A garage in Turin are coming out to look at it. But I think it is finished.'

'So what will you do?' asked Sophie.

Dieter clipped silently for a few moments. 'Don't know,' he said. 'Once you have taken as much of your harvest as possible, you will not need us.'

'Hey!' said Sophie. 'I won't just throw you out.' She sighed, staring down the valley. 'To be frank, I haven't thought beyond getting the harvest in. But that's only the start of the struggle. There is still such a lot to do.'

'Maybe I could stay and help,' Dieter said eagerly. 'For just a little time.'

He seemed very young. Vulnerable, for all his size.

'I'd be glad to have some company.' Sophie drew a green hand across her face. 'That goes for you and your parents, David,' she added. 'Thanks to all of you, I have got in three or four times what I could have harvested on my own.'

'But it's still not enough,' said David.

She clipped busily. 'Not really,' she answered quietly.

Could she pay off enough interest to persuade the bank to let her hang on for another year? Would they simply foreclose on her? If she had to turn to lawyers for help, how was she going to pay them? What if Brian had yet to sell off enough of his assets to pay the girls' boarding fees, as he had promised?

He had turned his back on stronger promises than that.

So many hurts and scars. A tear ran down Sophie's nose. She scrubbed at it, mixing white and green. Maybe the others would think it was only sweat — if they ever saw it. She struggled to take a firmer hold on her emotions.

'What's that?' asked David suddenly.

'What's what?' asked Dieter.

'Voices. Up in the mist.'

'It's hunger,' said Dieter. 'You are hallucinating.'

Then, above them on the slopes, they heard a woman's laughter. A man's deeper tone. Disembodied voices, drifting down through the thinning mist. The small hairs rose on Sophie's neck: it was as if all the spirits in the valley had come together, the past and the present bridged by this golden haze.

There was the sound of clay fragments,

rattling down the slopes between the trellises.

Down through the mist, came the valley people. In twos and threes. The women with their hair tied back by ribbons, or held by simple elastic bands. Others wearing straw hats, or old woolly ones, pulled down below their ears. Older men, their felt hats perched high on the back of their heads, and young men wearing baseball caps. Dark faces, used to toiling in the sun, people who had come to work, wearing old clay and grape-stained shirts and jeans and heavy skirts. Each of them carrying their share of empty crates.

In a ragged file, they came down through the trellises. Some smiled and waved. Some shouted over: '*Buongiorno, signora,*' or '*Buongiorno, Sophie.*'

Sophie stood, numbly, watching, tears leaving stark-white channels, down the green and brown stains on her face. She tried to wave, but her arm was too heavy. She tried to reply *Buongiorno*, but her heart was too full.

One older woman hesitated, then left the others. She came slowly through the vines, then reached out to touch Sophie's arm. 'I brought them back,' she said, in the French/Italian *patois* of the valley people.

'*Grazie, Maria,*' Sophie said huskily. She reached out with filthy arms, and hugged the woman who had been her housekeeper. And was still her friend.

Maria freed herself, tutted, and reached into a filthy anorak for a clean white tissue. She wiped the tears from Sophie's face. '*Prego*. And this time, as your mother would have done, I bring my own cutters. I will work with you. We will all work with you — as a way of saying that we are truly sorry.'

She glanced to where David and Dieter were standing wearily, stained with chemicals, shirts dark with sweat. 'It took two strangers to show the valley people what we should be doing,' she said. 'They shamed us, made us forget our pride.'

She looked directly at David and bowed slightly.

He looked embarrassed, then bowed back.

Dieter stretched huge arms above his head and punched air. 'We are single ants no longer,' he called over. 'We are a colony again. Together, working hard, we can save the vineyard yet . . . '

★　★　★

David struggled to lift and stack the heavy crates of grapes onto his trailer. The late morning sun streamed down, burning the bare skin of his arms and neck. Its warmth eased the weary muscles of his back.

With so many people harvesting, his job was now driving the tractor, ferrying the crates of fruit up to the cool darkness of the cellar, then bringing back fresh crates to fill. Heavy manual work that was oddly satisfying. It was years since he had felt so useful, so much *part* of something. He was sweating heavily, but it was as if the sweat had cleansed his soul.

Whistling, he reached down for another crate to load.

'Here. Let me help you.'

It was a young woman's voice. Scottish spoken. David wiped his eyes and peered against the sun. 'Kelly!' he said. 'Have I gone crazy? Is it really you?'

'I'll take this end. Now, *lift!*'

Between them, the crate flew high onto the trailer. He stared at his daughter.

'Gran and Granddad are up at the villa,' Kelly said. 'I made them breakfast, and chased Gran to bed. By the time I came downstairs, Granddad was fast asleep in one of the kitchen chairs. While I washed the dishes, I could hear voices, and women singing down here. So I followed the noise. Who are these people?'

'The valley folk,' David finally said. 'They've come, to help us.'

'Good,' she said. 'So I got here in time.'

'In time for what?'

'To help you too.'

'Dieter's right,' said David faintly. 'I *am* hallucinating.'

Kelly gripped another crate. 'These are heavy,' she said. 'Who is Dieter?'

David grunted as they swung the crate on board.

'Somebody else who turned up out of nowhere. What about your Master's studies back in Dundee?'

'What about your American sabbatical?'

Eyes sparkling, she challenged him over another crate of grapes. His first thought was how like her mother she looked. His second carried a twist of surprise: for the first time, comparing the two images brought no pain.

'OK,' he smiled. 'If I promise not to mention your Master's, then you don't mention my sabbatical. Peace?'

She solemnly shook his green-stained hand.

'Between us, always,' she said.

★ ★ ★

It was well into the night, but the three of them worked on. The electric press crushed the grapes that David and Sophie poured into it from the crates which had been filled that day while Sergio, one of Sophie's near-neighbours, was up the ladder, scrubbing and flushing clean another vat for them to fill.

'I can't believe it,' Sophie said quietly, her arms and face sprayed with grape juice and bits of purple skins. 'We will have eight vats at least, fermenting.'

'Enough to solve things, financially?' David was as grape-stained as herself, his shirt and jeans a write-off, and testament to a long day's work.

'Yes, and no,' said Sophie tiredly. 'It is a start.'

Together, they lifted another crate, and emptied it into the press. Sergio came down to collect the thick plastic hosepipe from the press, and carry it up to the freshly cleaned vat. Once he'd locked the hose in place, he descended again, a tireless worker, and switched on the small electric pump at the foot of the press. As it chattered, the level of juice and mulch in the trough dropped steadily.

They paused to watch it fall.

'The start of what?' asked David, glad of the break.

Sophie wiped splashes from her face. 'The race to my next hurdle. As the wine ferments, we must sample it at four week intervals. The wine control authority for the valley, must analyse and pass these samples. Then their tasting panel must pass the wine, once the vinification process is complete.'

'And if they don't pass it?' David asked.

'If we fail at any stage of the DOC approval, then I can't sell the wine as Nebbiolo from the valley. A top quality premium wine — the same grape as Barolo, only it hasn't been aged in oak barrels. And if I can't sell the wine . . . '

'Then all our work has been in vain?'

'Just about.'

David could sense her tension, and her exhaustion. Time to take her mind away from problems that were better considered on another day, when she was in a fresher state of mind to face them. 'When do you add the yeast?' he asked. 'I've been watching. Sergio's just filling vats, then moving on.'

'We don't use commercial yeast,' said Sophie. 'Everything that the wine needs — including yeast — is already in the juice, or fruit, or skins. These vats will be fermenting by tomorrow night. It's the most natural and self-contained process in the world. Essentially the same as when the Romans made their wine from these slopes, through many generations of people, in an unbroken chain. Sometimes, you can feel them watching you.'

David reached for another crate. 'Your Old

Ones,' he said. 'Dieter told me about them. And there is a feeling about this place. A presence. In my own work, history always leaves its shadows. Some for good. Some bad.'

Together, they lifted the crate, and spilled out its fruit.

Juice sprayed over them. He wiped his face. 'If they have guarded you up to now, then they won't desert you. Trust them. Somehow, you will get the approval that you need. Meanwhile, one step at a time. It looked a hopeless mess when we started. But we've got the tractor working, and the valley people back on board and helping you. Things are so much better than they were. Have faith.'

'I'll try. But it isn't easy. You don't know the half of it.'

'Then tell me tomorrow.'

'Maybe. It's all such a mess.'

Her head drooped. With every fibre of her being, she wanted to lie down, to give up the fight. Now that she had somehow got the harvest in, all the will and energy had simply drained from her. The thought of future problems was more than she could face — now, or later.

Sergio came over to stand beside them. He picked up some grapes, and felt them for firmness. Pulled a face. 'Too many soft fruits here.' Strong white teeth bit into one of the grapes. He chewed, then spat it out onto the floor. 'Too oily,' he muttered. 'We should have come here sooner. The valley people feel so guilty, Sophie. Our pride has cost you your harvest.'

'What did he say?' asked David.

'He's telling me what I know already,' said Sophie. 'We're in trouble. Even if we've got the harvest is in, there are too many soft grapes in it. Which will mess up the samples . . . '

'And DOC approval?'

She nodded miserably.

'Hey,' David said gently. 'Don't give up. You're tired, that's all. You've come so far — achieved the impossible. What you need right now is rest. Like I said, one step at a time. Let's finish the pressing, and get the wine fermenting. When we're fresher, we can think about the quality problems. You're not on your own any more — the valley people will do their best to help you. Forget about the mistakes that were made in the past. Start with a new clean sheet. Go cap in hand to them, and ask their advice. You said it yourself, they've been working here for centuries. They'll have made wine with duff grapes before. They'll know what to do.'

Sophie stared at him. He'd done it again.

Shown her the way forward — the only way with any chance of success was to link up again to the source of support that her ex-husband Brian had spurned as outdated and useless; directing her feet back to the one bridge she had known, throughout, was vital.

'What did he say?' asked Sergio.

'He says our only chance, is to ask your help,' said Sophie. 'He has a gift for plucking the truth out of thin air. We will never get the wine passed unless you show us how. Whatever Brian said in the past. For which, I am deeply sorry.'

'*Prego*. To be honest, I never liked the man. He was born to keep his fingers out of the clay. And you can't grow grapes with clean hands. You know that, Sophie, because you have always worked like a man. As this stranger has done.'

Sergio stared at David, measuring, judging. Then a slow smile spread over the sunburned face.

'If he wants our help, tell him he's got it,' he said quietly.

'What did he say?' asked David.

'I'll tell you tomorrow,' she said. 'For tonight, I'll just say 'thanks'.'

4

Sophie glanced up from setting the table at the sound of footsteps.

'Oh, it's you,' she said. 'I thought it was Dieter — he's usually the first to show for breakfast.'

'That's because he's German,' said David cheerfully. 'He can't stop himself from putting his towel over the best chair, before anybody else gets near the pool.'

Sophie laughed. 'We don't have a pool.'

David crossed over to the open kitchen door, and looked out at the crisp early morning sunshine in the courtyard. 'Another lovely day,' he said.

'It still feels strange,' Sophie said. 'Not rushing out to start cutting grapes at first light. It was so nice and fresh outside, I wanted to let the day come in. We're getting near the end of October. One of these mornings, it won't be summer sunshine any more. Only winter rain and mist.'

David leaned against the doorpost. The air was rich with the scent of the tall cedar trees around the villa. He could hear doves crooning, and the harsher sounds of distant magpies — as common in the wine valley as crows, back home.

Home. He stirred, uneasily. Harvesting was finished, and the vats of wine were fermenting in the cellars. Out there, the scent of living wine was strong enough to get you drunk. His usefulness here was over. He had helped when it was sorely needed. Now that was history. He was staying on merely to keep an eye on his parents, where Mary was getting more restive at being treated as an invalid with each passing day. He grinned: there was an explosion coming, if he knew his mother. It was time, he thought, to start planning to bring them home. Finish this strange adventure and drag everyone back to reality.

Yet it wasn't easy to turn and walk away. There was other, vital work still to do — and do quickly, not leaving things to drift. There had been too much marking time in the days following the harvest. Although he could understand, because the shadows of exhaustion were still on Sophie's face, and she clearly needed time to rebuild her energies. Making decisions hurt, but further decisions were needed. The crisis was over, but not the problem solved.

He sighed. Such a thin line between help and meddling.

'A big sigh,' she said. 'Problems?'

'My mum and dad,' he answered. 'We should be going home — this isn't a guest house. And I'm getting tired of fighting about who pays the bills for food.'

'Not a fight,' Sophie said briskly. 'You are my guests. I pay.'

'Mmm.'

At the cooker, she smiled. Only a Scot could write a book inside that grunt.

'Out with it,' she said. 'There's more than food bills bugging you.'

'True.'

'Well?'

'It's none of my business . . . '

Sophie brushed red hair aside. 'Mending my tractor wasn't your business. Cutting grapes wasn't your business. Bringing the valley people back onside wasn't your business. But it helped to save the vineyard. So why stop now?'

Turning from the door, David looked over guardedly. 'We really need to do something about that wine,' he said. 'Chase Sergio about his offer to help. All my instinct tells me that the sooner we start working on compensating for these over-ripe grapes, the better. The longer we leave it, the bigger the risk it will be too late, before we start.'

'There's plenty of time,' she said, busy in her kitchen.

'There's not.'

Her head snapped up. Irritation flared then died. His eyes were level, and he was only stating the truth as he saw it. The truth, as it was. Getting the harvest in had only been the first hurdle. She couldn't bring herself to face the next — finding a way to pass the stringent DOC controls. But hiding from the problem wouldn't solve it — and unsellable wine would only finalize her bankruptcy.

'Sorry,' David said. 'You have enough on your plate, without all of us hanging round your neck.'

'You're here as guests,' Sophie said firmly. 'Friends, who rolled up their sleeves and worked with me. When nobody else was there to help.'

'Volunteers, brought to you by the Old Ones,' he smiled. Backing off.

'Dieter sees it more as being press-ganged into helping by them.'

'And now our job is done.'

Sophie stood, her head bowed. 'Maybe it isn't,' she said quietly. 'I'm running scared. It helps to have people around me. Not just propping me up, but acting as a conscience too. You're right, we must do something about that wine. This morning we'll walk up the valley and ask Sergio. He'll tell us what to do. So, please stay a little longer. I've had enough of fighting on my own. I can still use your help.'

She looked up into the level, compassionate eyes. Strange, she could be so direct with this man. And with Dieter. They had worked together to achieve the impossible. Creating a bond which was forged on trust. On honesty.

'OK,' said David. 'Until you know what you're doing about the wine.'

'Will that mess up your own plans?'

'Not really. I'm on sabbatical. I should be over in America, doing research. It doesn't matter if I'm a few weeks late.'

Sophie busied herself at the cooker. 'Kelly says you don't want to go.'

'I don't,' said David. 'It's just . . . well, a change of scene.'

Young footsteps sounded outside the kitchen door. Kelly. She looked around the old kitchen. 'I love this room,' she said. 'It has such atmosphere. It's like the heart of the house. Did you buy the furniture locally, Sophie?'

'It came with the house,' said Sophie. 'It has been here for generations.'

'I thought so,' said Kelly. 'Where's Dieter? His bedroom door was open, but there's no sign of him. I thought he'd be down here, tucking into his breakfast.'

'He'd better turn up soon,' said David. 'Or we'll eat his share ourselves.'

91

★ ★ ★

'If only everybody would stop *fussing*,' Mary said crossly.

In their bedroom at Sophie's villa, where mid-morning sunshine streamed through the drawn-back curtains, Bert eyed her warily. He was restless to be out and doing something. Be of use to somebody. Anything other than hanging around, riding shotgun on the crabbiest stagecoach in the West. An active man, he hated these long days of idleness.

But he would have cut off a leg before he left Mary to herself.

'Who has been fussing?' he finally asked.

'Everybody,' Mary snapped. 'There's Kelly, in and out of here, treating me like her first-born who has whooping cough. Ramming me back into bed. We should never have bought her that nurse's uniform, when she was five.'

'She loves you,' Bert smiled. 'She came over here to look after you.'

'I don't *need* looking after,' Mary snarled. 'Then, there's David.'

Bert sighed. 'What's he done?'

'Sitting, watching me. Wondering if I'm ready for a granny farm.'

'There's none of them would take you,' Bert said.

'Just let him *try* to drag me home with him,' Mary said ominously.

Bert fidgeted. His buttocks felt as if they reflected every hump and hollow of the chair. 'Well, we can't stay here for ever,' he warned. 'It's not a boarding-house.'

'I don't want to stay here for ever.'

'Only until you're ready to be taken home.'

Her eyes drilled into him. 'Our home is out there, on four wheels.'

'You're not fit enough for the van,' he protested.

'I'm fit enough to sit and watch you drive. I'm fit enough to tell you what to buy, and how to cook the meals. In fact, there's nothing wrong with me. I'm fit enough to cook the meals myself. I want out. I want to be doing something.'

'In a day or two — '

'Now.' Mary rose. 'I'm going out to tidy up the van. I've never had a chance to clear things up, not since the flood. First, we were helping Sophie. Then I had that black-out thing.'

'You might kill yourself!' warned Bert.

Mary walked over, stared down. Then, prodding with a fingertip that hurt, she said slowly, 'Watch my lips, Bert. Because I'm only going to say this once, so you'd better get your head round it. I am not sitting here and waiting to die. I have a life to live, while I'm able and have the choice. I'm fine. Back to normal. I'm going down to clean and air the van. Then I'm telling Sophie that we will be leaving here, in a day or two. Going off to finish what we set out to do. Take the van south, crossing over into France from here — Dieter will tell us how. Then, following the sun down through France and into Spain. Like gypsies. Do you hear me, Bert?'

He blinked. 'The whole house heard you.'

'Good . . . ' A quiet knock on the door. 'Come in,' said Mary, gathering her strength to fight her corner if she had to. It was Sophie.

She looked at them uncertainly. 'I heard voices,' she said. 'I was trying to make up my mind about something. Wanted a second opinion.'

'Fire away,' said Mary, her belligerence gone as quickly as it had come.

'Where's David?' Bert asked. 'Has he disappeared, like Dieter?'

'I've left him talking wine-making up at Sergio's. With David's bad French, and Sergio's even worse English, they're down to drawing pictures and grunting.'

'Men are good at grunting,' Mary said.

'They seem to understand each other,'

Sophie sighed. 'It's a very male-oriented culture, here in the valleys. Men always talk to men, when it's business.'

'You wanted a second opinion,' Mary nudged.

Sophie walked over to the window, looking out at the sunlit yard.

'I had a crazy thought, while the two of them were talking.'

'Which was?'

Sophie stared out, unseeing. Then turned. 'It's nearly midterm, at my girls' school. I suddenly wanted to see them again, Let them know I miss them. Bring them back, for a few days' holiday.'

'What's so crazy about that?' Mary asked.

Sophie snorted. 'The airline tickets. I have barely enough money left to buy their return flights. Then I'm truly broke. So it's crazy, isn't it, spending my last dribble of money on letting them see the mess I'm making of the vineyard?'

'It's their mum they'll come to see, not the vineyard,' Mary said.

Sophie looked at Bert. 'Tell me it's daft,' she said.

'Hey!' said Mary. 'That's too much like your male-dominated culture thing.'

'I'm asking him as a friend, a man who thinks, but doesn't say very much.'

'I never get the chance,' grinned Bert. He

looked at her shrewdly. 'What is the most important thing in the world to you?' he asked.

'My girls,' Sophie answered. 'More important than the vineyard.'

'Then bring them over for their mid-term holiday,' Bert said.

'I could have told you that,' protested Mary.

★　★　★

The Langhe was the strangest and most beautiful place on Earth, Kelly thought. It was as if somebody had thrown a golden duvet carelessly over the countryside, leaving it lying in humps and folds. Tiny little villages with red roofs perched on top of the main hills, not down in the valleys, as in Scotland. And everywhere, as if a mathematician had sat down and calculated how to use every inch of land, leaving the maximum number of vines lying open to the sun, there were straight lines of trellises. Green vine leaves, bronze vine leaves. Vines everywhere.

While over everything, that wonderful Italian sun.

She wriggled her shoulders, warm and relaxed beneath her top. The dusty valley road wound up towards the high horizon.

Chalk dust puffed out beneath her marching feet. In the distance, she could hear a dog begin to bark. Its warning was taken up by other dogs, in other vineyards, spreading like ripples across the surface of a lazy pool.

Kelly stopped at a bend on the narrow road. Turned to face the sun. She closed her eyes, threw back her head, and opened her arms wide, bathing in the golden heat and light as if it was a magic shower. Time slowly stopped.

A man's cough. Startled, she spun round, feeling foolish.

'You looked like a statue,' said Dieter. 'Why does your skin never tan?'

'It never has done.' It was too beautiful a day to feel embarrassment. She smiled up at him. Despite his size, he was the least threatening man she had ever met. A gentle giant. 'Where have you been all day?' she demanded. 'We thought you'd run away and left us.'

Dieter shrugged. 'I went for a walk,' he said.

Kelly glanced at her watch. 'But that was almost ten hours ago.'

'It was a long walk.'

'Where did you go?'

'Here and there. Up into the hills.'

'The others are starting to get worried.'

Dieter looked uncomfortable. 'I didn't know it was going to be a long walk when I left,' he said. 'It's just that sometimes . . .'

She waited, but he seemed to have retreated to some place deep inside his mind. 'Sometimes what?' she asked.

He started slightly. As if he'd drifted away from her. From everything.

'It's not important,' he said.

'Try me?'

He smiled sheepishly. 'OK, but you will think that I am crazy. Sometimes, I have to get away from people. From houses. Be on my own for a bit. Come back when I am tired, or hungry. When I had the van, I had nobody to worry about but myself. If I wanted to go — like the Aborigines say — walkabout, then I walked. I have been a lot on my own. It is like a drug. The silence.'

Kelly dropped in step beside him and they walked slowly back down the rolling hills towards the valley bottom again. 'That's not crazy,' she said, at last. 'We all need privacy at times. A chance to think.'

'Exactly.'

'Will you buy another campervan?'

'I haven't decided. It was good for me, these last eight months. Perhaps now, I should be staying somewhere. Committing, instead of drifting.'

'Going home?'

The German stopped in his tracks. 'Not that,' he said quietly. 'Not yet.'

'I know what you mean,' smiled Kelly. 'I want to take a year out. See a bit of the world before I start to do more serious work. Find a place where I can help people. Maybe in Africa. Maybe in South America.'

'There are many people needing help. Beneath many coloured skins.'

'I know that,' Kelly said.

'Of course you do.'

As their stride pattern quickened into a proper walking rhythm, she found herself telling the huge figure at her side all of her hopes and dreams. Her hatred of a society where people fought for power and greed. Her fear that the world was being pillaged, emptied and destroyed to satisfy that greed. Her hope that one day she would find a job to do where there was no pollution, no ripping out of scarce reserves, no greed for mindless profits. No collateral damage, anywhere.

'It's naïve,' she finally said. 'Simply a dream.'

'It needn't be.'

'What's your dream?' Kelly asked. A long

silence. 'Come on,' she said. 'It's your turn to bare your soul.'

'I have no dream,' said Dieter.

Kelly waited, but the only sound was their heels against the dusty road.

'You don't give away much,' she teased.

Dieter smiled. 'Some of us are born to listen.'

★ ★ ★

Even in the era of the mobile phone, it was standard security at the boarding-school that all calls went through the school office. Sophie waited, tapping her fingers.

'Moorhurst College.'

'Sophie Hargreaves here. I would like to speak to my daughters, Sara and Hannah, please.'

'Is it an emergency?'

No. It is just a little time since they last phoned home. I thought if I waited until after lessons and homework . . . '

'Of course. I will ask the girls to return your call.' Another security shield. 'You are at your home number, Mrs Hargreaves?'

'Yes.'

'Then, thank you. The girls will soon be in touch, from this office.'

The line went dead. Sophie sagged back

against the chair, letting her breath out in one long sigh. No demands that she should pay the school fees. Brian must have kept his promise to handle them. Just as well: in her entire life, she had never been so tight for cash before. It felt degrading. Destroyed her self belief.

'Are you all right, Sophie?'

It was Dieter, passing through the hall.

Sophie grimaced. 'I'm waiting for my daughters to phone. And I'm scared.'

He towered above her, smiling. 'What did Maria say to you? About wiping her sons' noses when they were young, so why should she fear them now?'

'If only it was that simple,' Sophie sighed. 'Maria doesn't have to cope with the baggage of a marriage that has broken down.'

'Baggage?'

'Burden. Weight of guilt. Fear that my girls still blame me for it happening.'

Dieter laid a gentle finger on her shoulder. 'Courage, Sophie,' he said. 'It is the law of nature that parents will be blamed for everything.'

'How do you know that?'

'Because I blamed my parents too. It is a form of love.'

Sophie laughed. Dieter and David were good for her. Their gentle humour had the magic touch to lift her mood. She enjoyed their company. In this endless grind of worry, they were always there to lean on when she needed them. And, independent woman though she was, she'd had her fill of toughing it out alone.

'I need to wait out here,' she said. 'Are the others in the kitchen?'

He nodded. 'I am going there to help Mary win her battle.'

'Which battle is that?'

'She wants to get back on the road in her van, now that she's fit again.'

'Could they cope on their own, she and Bert?'

'They did before.'

'What if she gets sick again?'

'Why should she?'

'It will be over David and Kelly's dead bodies,' Sophie warned.

'That is my job,' sighed Dieter. 'To resolve the dispute without too many casualties.' A shadow crossed his face. '*Insha Allah*,' he added quietly

'God willing,' she translated automatically.

'Exactly. We are insects moving towards the destiny He has set for us.'

'A sombre thought. Who told you that?'

'A wise man. Dying.'

'Oh.' Like many of the German's conversations, this had reached a point from which there was no obvious route ahead. The phone rang. 'That will be my daughters,' Sophie said, thankfully.

'Then I will go. Good luck. And remember, Sophie: one day their children will blame them too . . . '

It drew the intended smile. Sophie picked up the phone. 'Hello,' she said.

'Mummy? It's Sara. What's wrong? Why are you phoning?'

'Nothing's wrong,' said Sophie. 'I just wanted to hear your voice again.'

'What happened with the harvest, Mummy? Did you get it in?' Out of her two girls, Sara was the one who shared Sophie's passion for the vines.

'Most of it. Some people, strangers, dropped in to help. And the valley folk came back, for a morning, too.'

'I'm so glad,' Sara said. 'They were so good to us, to start with. Daddy was wrong to chase them all away.'

Sophie bit her tongue. A broken marriage wasn't helped when one condemned the other. 'Have you any plans for the mid-term holiday?' she asked.

'Not really. Hannah is maybe going down to Dorset with her friend. I was thinking of visiting Daddy, in London. But he's too busy.'

The hurt in her voice triggered slow-burning anger in Sophie. Nothing had changed: Brian spoiled Hannah, and took little interest in Sara. Too much like her mother — not bright enough. She swallowed. 'How would you both like to fly over to Turin? I could collect you at the airport.'

'I'd love to,' Sara said instantly, her voice excited. 'Is the wine fermenting?'

'Going strong. How about Hannah? Is she — ?'

A new voice on the phone, cool and poised against the uncertainty that surrounded Sara like a cloud. 'Hannah can speak for herself,' it said.

'Hi, Hannah. How are you?' Sophie asked.

'I'm good.'

Sophie winced at the Americanism. 'Would you like to come — ?'

'I heard,' Hannah said. 'Is Daddy going to be there?'

'No. Sorry, my love. That's over. Finished.'

'I thought so. Look, would you mind if I stayed here? We're going to do some sailing in Anna's dinghy if the weather stays fine.'

Sophie couldn't push. Not when she was walking a tightrope, trying to help them adjust to the ruins of their early life. 'Of course,' she said. 'Not a problem.'

'Sara can manage on her own.'

The voice was calm, assured. Thirteen, going on thirty. Her father's daughter.

'Of course she can.'

''Bye, Mummy. Keep well.'

Sophie heard the phone being handed over. The sound of footsteps leaving the school's office. Then her elder daughter's breathing, her insecurity a tangible thing, flowing down the phone. The casualty of a very bright father, and a younger sister who outshone her effortlessly at school.

'Sara here, Mummy. Will you still want to see me on my own? There's plenty for me to do over here. If it's easier, I can stay.'

'You will do no such thing,' Sophie said firmly. 'And I can't imagine anybody I would rather have beside me for a few days than you.'

Silence. Then a sniff. 'All right then, Mummy.'

'Good,' said Sophie. 'I'll organize the ticket, and send it over to the school.'

''Bye, Mummy,' said Sara quietly. 'Love you.'

'Love you too.'

★ ★ ★

The morning mist drifted through the narrow streets of the old hill village. Sophie drew into

105

one of the few empty parking spaces outside a low, functional concrete building. Most were cluttered with the locals' tiny APE vans — three-wheeled and canvas-sided vans built round the front wheel and handgrips of a motorbike. A mud-spattered Mercedes estate waited, its tailgate sagging low with wine. Someone touring the wine roads, dropping in to sample and buy.

Behind her, the rear door opened. 'Give me a minute,' Sergio said. 'I will go and speak to him first. Tell him what the problems were with your vines.'

'*Grazie, Sergio.*'

'*Prego.*'

The Fiat door slammed shut, and they watched Sergio's square, powerful figure heading up the steps and into the wine producers' co-operative.

'Are you sure you need me here?' asked David. 'I don't speak the language.'

'That's not important,' Sophie said. 'You're here for business reasons. In rural *Piemonte*, it is a man's culture. When there's business to be done, men talk to men. The co-operative manager wouldn't feel comfortable, talking to me.'

'But — '

'I will translate.'

David scratched his head ruefully. 'So I'm

here as a ventriloquist's dummy?'

'Just about. I'll be careful not to tickle, when I'm working you.'

They both laughed. It was the difference of having real support beside her, Sophie thought. Your nerves spilled out in easy banter, leaving you stronger and more determined to face the task ahead.

'I'm still surprised that Sergio agreed to go for technical help,' David said.

'Why? Your argument was sound. If the problem lies outside the valley people's experience, it makes sense to turn to experts. Because most of the locals are small growers rather than wine producers. Sure, they keep some grapes to make a little wine for themselves. But not to sell commercially. They have good working knowledge — but they don't have to pass the DOC tests. That's why Sergio said that you fight fire with fire, so you must fight scientific testing with a scientist.'

She sighed. 'You've more than paid your way already. He listened to your idea, and thought hard about it. Because it came from a man. Not me.'

'Maybe. So this is the producers' co-operative he uses himself?'

'He's been bringing his grapes here for years. He says the manager is the most knowledgeable man in the valleys, and that he will surely help us.' Sophie glanced at her watch. 'Sergio has had long enough. Let's go in now.'

They walked up the steps, pushing through the doors into a building that was more a warehouse than an office. The smell of wine was everywhere, from the cellars outside, the scarred table of opened bottles and empty glasses from earlier tastings and the cases of wine which were stacked to the ceiling. It was cold enough inside, to make you shiver — new wine must be kept cool. In the far corner, Sergio was talking to a small, wiry man in his late thirties, perched easily on the edge of a desk that was overflowing with papers. Dressed in jeans and an open-necked check shirt, he looked more like a worker than a manager.

Then the eyes flicked up at their approach. Dark, intent, intelligent. He came over, hand outstretched. 'Hi. I'm Guiseppe. Call me Joe. Sergio tells me that you're facing some pretty major issues with your wine.'

'You speak English!' Sophie exclaimed.

'More like American. I lived over there for three years, while I took my Master's. Sergio says you over-fertilized the vines last harvest, and were too late in getting in the grapes for this one.'

Sophie winced. While there was no condemnation in his voice, the stark facts made it sound as if she was only playing with her vines. And doing it badly. 'I'm here to ask for help. To see if you can find a way of getting this year's wine through the sample tests and the DOC tasting panel.'

'Yes, and no. Won't know for sure until your wine is sampled and we see the numbers. There could be a fertilizing hangover — you should have tested your soil in spring, checking its mineral balance. But vines are greedy feeders. They probably binged on fertilizer last year, and have self-corrected. How was last year's wine?'

'Thin, acidic, horrible,' said Sophie. 'A disaster, like the valley people warned us it would be.'

Guiseppe nodded. 'The fertilizer would make the vines fruit too much and leave the grapes too big, maybe even with mineral traces in their flesh. But that was last year. The soil should be better this year. If so, then the main problem is simply your late harvesting this season.'

'Can we correct for that?' David asked.

Guiseppe nodded. 'It's possible. But only after close analysis. And only with a top bio-chemist helping, because you're way beyond my help, right now. Way beyond what

Sergio and the valley guys can offer. You need hand-holding from a vinification consultant, working alongside him to balance your wine.'

'Where can we find a man like that?' Sophie asked.

'I know a guy,' said Guiseppe. 'The man we use ourselves — along with all the other big producers. If we can get Paulo helping you, he can work miracles on the wine while it is still growing. He's on half a dozen DOC panels. But he's not involved with *Nebbiolo D'Alba*, so there won't be a conflict of interest. He's your man, if you can interest him.'

'All the top producers use him?' Sophie asked.

'Yup. *Barolo, Barbaresco, Barbera* . . . the whole way through the alphabet, covering every grape we grow inside these valleys.'

'Then he'll charge a lot of money,' she said dismally.

'He's a fair guy. I know him well — we were sent over to America together by our parents. Sworn to keep each other out of trouble. The only trouble I had with Paulo was dragging him out of college libraries and restaurants. He was a gross feeder, on both counts. Even now, his wife keeps him on a permanent diet — be warned, his first act will be to drag you into a four-hour business

110

lunch. But he knows everything there is to know about making wine. He'll look at your problem, analyse. He won't waste your money. He'll tell you straight from the shoulder if he can turn the situation round, or not. If it's possible, he'll draw up a programme of working with you over the next three months and estimate the likely cost.'

Sophie turned to David. 'There's no way I can afford a man like that!'

In her mind had been the blind, almost childlike, hope that the producers' co-operative would offer to help her out of the goodness of their heart, and show her a simple way in which she could correct the wine, making it good enough to pass the testing. This was her reality check. She felt panic rising.

'Find out if the problem is solvable first,' David answered quietly. 'Then sort out the money issues. If you don't get help, then you have no wine to sell. And, if you don't have wine to sell . . . '

Sophie bit her lip. She was used to working with the living vines, not making decisions like this. Handling strategy. Balancing risks. That had been Brian's job, but he had let her down. Now, she could only add his burden to her own. Silence filled the long warehouse

111

building. Outside, the sound of someone whistling.

Sergio stirred. 'Trust in God, Sophie,' he said. 'In God, and the Old Ones.'

Guiseppe added, in Italian. 'A problem sometimes changes when you come at it in a different way. You're worrying that you can't afford to hire Paulo. What you should be asking yourself is this: can you afford *not* to hire him?'

'What did they say?' asked David, urgently.

'The same as you. They said I don't have any choice.'

'Then go for it. Between the three of us, we'll come up with a way of raising the money. Surely.'

She stared at him. If Sergio was right, he and Dieter had been sent to her by the Old Ones to help her find a way out of this unending mess.

Her shoulders squared. Sophie would never be short on courage.

'Right. How do we contact this Paulo?' she asked Guiseppe.

5

Sophie had loved this kitchen from the moment she set eyes on it — in what now seemed a different life. A big airy room, with ancient dark furniture, a long oak table, a stone fireplace where burning logs sent spirals of sparks up the chimney and, above everything, the old yellowed clock with its heavy tick measuring time and centuries. The heartbeat of the house.

She had moved here to fulfil a dream, where she would one day sit and smile to watch the different generations of her family. Now the table was ringed with someone else's family, strangers who had made her plight their own.

Which didn't stop them squabbling, as families always do.

'I still think you're crazy,' Kelly hissed.

Mary shrugged. 'Think what you want. We're going.'

Despite her problems, Sophie smiled. Kelly and her grandparents functioned as three equals, the age gap ignored. It was never clear who was looking after whom. Their bond was so intense, and possessive, that David must have felt left out at times. He looked over to her now and raised a wry eyebrow.

What was supposed to be a brain-storming session for herself, David and Dieter had quickly become a family debate. Everyone had ideas of how she could raise the money to pay for Paulo, the wine consultant. He had come, sampled, blown out his cheeks — then returned late that same night, with sheets of scribbled paper outlining the corrections they must make on an almost daily basis, over the next few weeks. He, David and Sergio had disappeared out to the cellars until well after midnight. Then David came back wearily, to say, 'We've started. Paulo showed us how.'

Time was so vital, they had to act first, then worry about how to pay Paulo's much-discounted bill later. He had waved away down payments. Sophie could pay when she had raised the cash, he said dismissively. Now, they were discussing ways and means.

'I am not borrowing money from anyone here,' Sophie repeated firmly.

From around the dark-oak table, they stared back at her.

'OK,' said Mary. 'I have a better idea. You've loads of empty bedrooms in this huge old house. Convert two or three of them into modern en-suite guest rooms. Then offer bed and breakfast for tourists coming along the wine roads throughout the year.'

Kelly nodded. 'Not crazy,' she said. 'If it's anything like home, the Italian Tourist Board will be giving grants and cheap loans for any improvements to accommodation that would bring more visitors.'

'Building workers cost a fortune,' Sophie protested.

'Not with Tourist Board help,' said Mary.

'You don't need building workers,' Dieter said eagerly. 'Use the Tourist Board money to buy new toilets, showers, pipes and plaster boarding. I could stay on here and build these in for you. I am good with work like this.' He looked up the table pleadingly. 'Honest. I can do it.'

Sophie's eyes stung. How often, over the centuries, had a family sat around this table and pooled their wits and energies to keep the vineyard going? She had imagined it would be her own daughters, and their children. Not this strange and varied family that the Old Ones had brought to her.

'David?' she said desperately. 'What do you think?'

David nodded. 'Not a bad long-term idea. It's like our whisky trails, you have year-round tourism. But you'd still need what you haven't got — up-front money to buy materials. And your earnings from visitors would come flowing in too late for Paulo's payment.'

'And where would I find the time, to run and B and B?'

'Maria,' Kelly said. 'She kept house for you before. She would come back and handle the visitors, if you asked. The main problem is the up-front money.'

'The bank will give you money,' Dieter said. 'We go back and bargain with them. Tell them, if they help us to pay for Paulo, then we will save the vintage and pay off your loan. If they refuse, you and they will lose everything. Use Paulo's local reputation to lever extra funds.'

Instant silence round the table: this was an idea that could work.

'Like Guiseppe said,' Sophie muttered, 'if you come at a problem in a different way, you see a different solution. But would the bank listen to me?'

'You need a man to front the deal,' Dieter said. 'Let me come with you and handle the negotiations. That was my work before . . . ' His face clouded.

Sophie glanced at David. 'What do you think?'

'A great idea. You're always complaining that men talk to men, on business — so use that, rather than fight it. But you want a Plan

B too. A way to bring in money quicker. This wine we've been drinking every night. Is it yours?'

'It's the very first vintage we made, with the valley people helping, before we ruined the grapes with over-fertilization. The DOC tasting panel failed us, but Sergio said that was about politics, and not the wine. They saw Brits coming here to play at making wine, and wanted to warn us that the district's reputation was a serious one. So they fired a shot across our bows. Despite the wine being OK.'

'And there's plenty of it?' David asked.

'A full harvest. Over 20,000 bottles.'

'That's a major asset. Why did you never sell it?'

'It didn't have the DOC approval to be released as *Nebbiolo D'Alba*.'

David picked up his near-empty glass and swirled the wine gently up its sides. 'It looks good and it tastes good,' he said slowly. 'Better than a lot of French wine that costs a fortune. Why not label it, and sell it as *vino da tavola* — table wine. In any restaurant, the house wine is usually only good quality table wine. Can you make up a brand name, get a label designed, and sell it as that?'

'I don't know,' Sophie said wretchedly. 'The whole marketing side was Brian's job.

But he wanted top quality from the start. So that first vintage has been gathering dust down in the underground cellars.'

'We could ask Paulo,' David mused. 'Or Guiseppe. They would know.'

'How would we sell it?' Sophie asked.

'Pay someone in Britain to take sample crates around Italian restaurants,' David said. 'Let the owners taste the wine. Try to strike a deal with them — anything you get is turning an idle asset into cash. Then ship the orders over. How do you send crates of wine from here?'

'I don't know,' said Sophie.

'Guiseppe must export wine. We can ask him, tomorrow.'

'Sophie, let me help,' said Kelly. 'There's no need to pay a stranger who has no commitment to your cause. I'll go round the restaurants for you. If it works. Dad's right, you're generating cashflow. And if it doesn't, then you won't have to find wages on top of your other costs.'

'What about your Master's?' David demanded.

Defiantly, she stared across the table at him.

He grinned. 'I forgot. Our pact that if I didn't mention your Master's, then you wouldn't mention my sabbatical. Sorry.'

'Well, Sophie? You were looking for ideas,'

Kelly said. 'Now you've got them — a whole programme to put your vineyard back on its feet. A short-term strategy to raise cash through selling wine; a long-term strategy to convert some bedrooms and take in tourists. What about it?'

'So many ideas. I don't know what to think,' said Sophie.

'Go for it,' said Mary. 'What do you have to lose?'

★ ★ ★

'I wonder how they're getting on,' said Mary.

'Who?' Bert hauled the van round a tight corner in the narrow road. At least driving on the right kept him away from the edge. Some bits of the coastal route they'd followed for three days, were downright scary. He'd be glad when they were inland, and on better roads south. 'Who?' he asked again, as Mary day-dreamed.

'David and the others. That Paulo's clever — designing the label himself and getting it printed. When are they trucking out the wine?'

'Yesterday, I think. Kelly was to go ahead, and wait for it at David's place.'

'Will it be safe there? The wine?'

'Safer than storing it in Kelly's flat,' Bert grinned.

They left the coast and began to climb through the pine trees.

'Such lovely hill country,' Mary said contentedly. 'I always wanted to see the Côte d'Azur and Marseilles. It never dawned on me that the Mediterranean was just down the road from where Sophie lives.'

'Uh-uh,' said Bert, slowing behind a lorry belching smoke. On these narrow roads with their blind bends and hairpins, how was he going to get past? 'Can you see ahead, if I edge out a bit?' he asked.

'No!' Mary shouted, as a sports car flashed downhill.

'Now I know why people get left-hand drive if they're doing a lot of touring on the Continent,' Bert mumbled. His shirt was sticking to him. Everyone drove like crazy here, much faster than back home.

Mary coughed, as the lorry's diesel exhaust filtered into the cab. 'Now!' she said, as Bert eased out again, then closed her eyes when he swung round the tail of the lorry and floored the accelerator. 'Are we still alive?' she asked, a little later.

'Just about,' said Bert, dropping in front of the lorry and easing off speed.

Mary watched the trees recede below them,

then the open plains of French countryside sprawl out in front. 'We've had nice campsites, up to now. Where are we stopping tonight?' she asked.

'The place we booked into this morning.'

'How far to go?'

'You're the navigator. Check the map. It's in the door pocket at your side.'

'OK, I'll look,' said Mary, without enthusiasm.

His tension easing with the more open landscape and the straighter roads, Bert watched wryly as she found the page, then turned it one way, then the other. 'I've marked where we're heading for,' he prompted. 'It's got a French name.'

'Why not? It's in France,' she said.

'Very funny. Never mind the town names. Do you see where the road breaks away from the coast? We're about an inch along that, by now . . . so how many inches are left to where I've circled?'

'Dunno,' she said.

'Come on,' he said impatiently. 'If I stop at a lay-by to look, that lorry could get past me again. From memory, there's about six or seven to go on the map — around fifty miles. But I've been driving for three hours . . . I'm punchy.'

'We need to find a supermarket and stock up,' Mary said.

'First we need to find the campsite that we're looking for,' he said crossly.

A dirty white van passed them, hesitated, then sped on.

'Bert,' Mary said uncertainly. 'That van has passed us a couple of times already. I recognize the rust on its rear door . . .'

'It's probably going off the main road and delivering,' Bert said. 'Look, try to concentrate on the map. We're about an inch in from where it leaves the coast . . . so how many inches further, to where it's marked on the map?'

Mary turned the map round. 'Maybe ten inches,' she said.

'It can't be. We're closer than that.'

Mary's head snapped round, as they passed a side road.

'Bert,' she said. 'There's that van again. I'm sure it's the same one . . .'

'So what?' Bert said tiredly. 'It's obviously dropping stuff off at all the farms along the way. Look, I'm going to have to stop at the next lay-by. Take a look at the map myself. Have a cup of tea. Stretch my legs and breathe some fresh air.'

He yawned, scrubbing his face with one hand. 'Keep your eyes on the road ahead,' he said. 'Shout, if you see a lay-by sign.'

* * *

'Hello. Can I watch, please?'

On his knees and stripping down the engine of Sergio's APE van, David glanced up. It was Sara, Sophie's daughter, over on her mid-term break. Such a shy girl: even her voice sounded more like a younger child.

'Of course you can,' he said. 'But beware oil. It's everywhere.'

Sara edged in, standing some distance away. For a while, she watched in a silence broken only by the noise of metal on metal, as David dismantled the tiny engine. Then she said, 'Mummy can't believe that Sergio asked you to service his van. That's a great honour. This is Sergio's most prized possession.'

'It's maybe an honour, but it's also a challenge,' David sighed.

A pause. 'Why's that?' As if she had weighed up whether or not the question would annoy him, before she asked.

'I've never worked on a two-stroke engine before.'

Another pause. Curiosity won. 'Then how will you ever manage to put it together again?' she asked.

'Simple,' David said. 'You always strip an engine down systematically, and that shows you how things are fitted and held together. The trick is to lay them out properly, then

123

assemble them in reverse order.'

'I'd never have thought of that,' she said. No pause this time.

'That's because you've never had a car. So you've never been curious and tried to find out how it works.'

'Is that not just for boys?'

'Why? It's not rocket science. And it saves money if you're running an old banger, like most of us start out with.'

David began to work again. Silence, while she watched. He felt so sorry for her: these shy silences were self-destructive, a barrier. He groped behind for a spanner he had laid aside. Felt it put quietly into his hand. She'd edged closer.

'Watch the oil,' he warned.

'Too late,' Sara said. 'Which part is that? What are you doing with it?'

Thirty seconds later, she was in the tiny cab at his shoulder, holding tools, and passing them to him when he asked. Her hands were soon as filthy as his own. As he changed the plugs on the little engine, David explained how they worked. Traced where the fuel came down, was vaporized, lit by a controlled spark into a contained explosion that drove a piston. Showed her how the piston's movement was converted into power. Her fair hair fell down beside his own dark hair. The intensity of her interest, a list of questions in its own right.

A lifelong teacher, David recognized an active mind and was happy to fill it gently with a drip-feed of facts and explanations. He sensed her excitement as she began to see how the tiny engine worked to drive its usually overloaded van.

Wiping his hands on waste cloth, he offered it to Sara. 'Get the worst off on that,' he said. 'I have some Swarfega here. It breaks down the oil, and cleans your hands before you wash them.'

Sara scrubbed at her hands. 'That consultant, what is he doing to get our wine right? Is he using chemicals to correct the balance?'

Her mind was already back on the vinery: her mother's daughter.

'He's only allowed to use natural elements,' David answered. 'Modern versions of the ancient cures they always used. Some of these were pretty gruesome. For some problems, they killed a cockerel and threw it into the vat. They didn't know why this worked — only that it always did — '

'And they still drank the wine?' Sara interrupted incredulously.

'They'd fish out the carcass, or whatever, and filter the wine. Then let the fermentation die naturally, by throwing open their cellar doors to winter cold.'

'Is Paulo putting dead birds into our wine?' she demanded.

'Not quite. But bio-chemistry has worked out *why* these old cures always worked . . . by neutralizing, compensating. Now they've developed a whole range of natural powders and essences that have the same effect. Paulo's drawn up a schedule, to feed in a little of this, or that, then leave it to work.'

'Can I watch?'

'You can help. So long as you promise not to fall off the ladder and into a vat — that's more drastic than killing cockerels.'

'Can we do it now?' The girl's eyes were shining.

'There's Sergio's van to finish. I have to give it a run and check everything's working OK. Then take it back up the valley to him.'

'Can I come?'

'There's no room in the cab — it's a motor bike, really.'

'I meant in the back.'

'If you don't fall out.'

'I won't.' She scrambled inside, before he had the chance to offer help.

Anger grew inside him. In all his teaching life, he had never met a child so desperate for company yet so afraid that she would only annoy people. Who had distorted her like this? Because Sara's special skill was making sure that she never got under anyone's feet. A survival skill, honed to Olympic standard inside the very family who should have been giving her security.

He began to search slowly through his pockets.

'What are you looking for?' she asked finally, when he thought the gambit had failed. 'The keys? They're in the ignition.'

'Bananas,' he said. And waited.

'What for?' Curiosity defeated uncertainty.

'It's an APE van,' he explained. 'You've got to feed it first. Before you start.'

Silence. Then a gurgle of laughter. He found himself laughing too.

'For a moment, I thought you were serious,' Sara said.

Silently, from the shadows of the doorway, Sophie watched. She'd come to be on hand to offer help, in what she knew might be an awkward situation. Her shy daughter feared men, because she had learned to dread Brian's impatience and ridicule. Instead, David had handled the situation brilliantly — and naturally. The two of them were now firm friends. She smiled.

For once, it was nice not to be needed.

★ ★ ★

Bert glanced from the map, as a white van swung into the lay-by in front of him, then reversed, blocking the space he needed for his own exit. People had no courtesy.

'Bert,' Mary said. 'It's that van again. I'm scared.'

Bert hesitated. They were sitting at the table in the van's sitting-room, well away from the cab. There was a boiling kettle and cups and packets of biscuits spread over the cooker and the serving surfaces. Rushing forward and starting the engine for a quick get-away simply wasn't an option.

'It's the first lay-by in miles. They're probably taking a break too,' he said. 'We'd never give them a second thought, if it was back in Britain.'

Frowning, he went forward and pushed down the cab-door locks, sealing themselves in. Mary's unease was catching. They were out in the middle of nowhere in open countryside, miles from the main road south. Traffic was light, now that they had left the coast behind. Fine for driving, but . . . Peering through his windscreen, Bert wished for a clogged-up British road, the bow-waves of wind made by passing lorries, rocking his van.

Ahead, the white van lurched, and a couple of men in overalls, came from either side.

One stretched his arms above his head and yawned. The other glanced up and down the empty road, then headed towards them.

He saw Bert at the windscreen, and pointed urgently down to the tyre at the back of the campervan, shouting something as he approached.

A slow puncture? Something wrong with the wheels? Bert reached to open the cab door.

'Don't!' Mary shouted. He felt her come up behind him. 'Don't open the door to these men, Bert. There's something wrong about them.'

Outside, the man rapped impatiently on the cab window, gesturing for Bert to get out. He shouted again, pointing back at the rear tyre repeatedly. Knocked the window angrily.

Dark, long hair that didn't look too clean. A sunburned skin, with stubble.

He could be a Good Samaritan. Or a mugger. Bert didn't know which and wasn't ready to find out the hard way. 'Go back through the van and make sure the habitation door is locked,' he hissed at Mary. 'I'll drop the cab window down an inch, and hear what he has to say . . . '

He wound the window down a little. Outside, the man gestured for him to open further. Bert shook his head. 'What's wrong?' he called out.

'*Ouvrez. Vite.*' Then a string of French that was too fast, for Bert to follow.

'Don't speak the language,' Bert said. Keeping well back. The man slammed the flat of his hand against the window. Shock tactics.

'Eemergensay! Out, you! Fast!'

They were in serious trouble. Desperately, Bert tried to see round the van parked hard against him, praying for traffic approaching down the empty road. The second man came down the other side, and began to try the caravan door. When that wouldn't open, he, too, began to hammer at it with the flat of his hand.

The noise boomed inside the campervan. Like being inside a drum.

'Phone for help!' Mary called.

'Who?' Bert asked. Then his mind clicked into gear. He was suddenly calm, knew exactly what must be done. Mary saw the certainty push indecision from his face. 'Here, lass,' he said. 'Take the mobile. Sit here in the front and pretend you're phoning out.'

'Where are you going?' she asked.

'The wardrobe. For the tyre-changing bag,' said Bert.

'You're not going outside!' she shouted.

'I want the big tyre lever,' Bert said,

throwing clothes aside. 'If they see me with that . . . they'll maybe think twice about breaking in.'

'They'll kill you!'

'Not until I've broken a couple of wrists, or heads,' he said grimly.

'Bert!'

'Look,' he said calmly, 'I was brought up in the toughest council house estate in Edinburgh. If a couple of Frenchies think I'm helpless, they can think again.'

'Can they get in?' she demanded, as the robbers gave up pretence, and started wrenching at the doors.

'We're safe enough,' he lied.

They weren't. If these were professional thieves, their next move would be to attack the rear window which was simply thin, double-skinned acrylic — not even glass. Standard caravan double-glazing, designed to keep out the cold, not protect them in a siege. Two slices of a Stanley knife, and the robbers could be in. It would leave him with only seconds to discourage them. A broken wrist might make the second thief hesitate. Once they were inside, he would be helpless. His only option was to keep them out. Defiantly, Bert waited for the attack.

In the distance, coming up the road he had just travelled, he saw two campervans approaching. How could he attract attention?

Bert racked his brains. To go out and wave them down, was to abandon the safety of their castle; to stay inside, and wave through the rear window, might only be taken as a friendly act. Didn't motorhomers always wave, when they passed each other?

To his relief, the first van slowed while the would-be robbers went back to lean nonchalantly against their own van, lighting cigarettes, feigning two vehicles sharing a lay-by and taking a break.

Bert beckoned feverishly through the rear window.

The first van slid in behind and stopped. The second drew up, alongside, part-blocking the road. Bert heard cab doors slam closed, and scrambled forward to unlock and open his own door.

'Hi, there. Trouble?'

'You bet,' said Bert. 'I've never been so glad to see a couple of motorhomes.'

'You didn't let them into your van?'

'No chance,' said Bert.

'Come on then — no, hang onto that iron lever. If we don't look tough, we'll never bluff them out . . . '

A squeal of air brakes and, for the first time, the two would-be robbers looked uneasy. A huge continental lorry had drawn up on the road, aware that something had happened, possibly an accident. Its driver looked out and shouted. The first of Bert's rescuers pointed at the two from the dirty white van and mimed an attempt to break into the parked campervan. The lorry driver nodded and slid down.

The two thugs headed round to their own cab. One threw up his hand in an angry, dismissive gesture, as he stepped inside. The van's engine roared and it lurched out of the lay-by, spraying stones.

'*Merci bien*,' Bert said to the lorry driver.

'*Prego*.' An Italian, who probably spent his life on other countries' roads. The lorry's big engine rumbled, and it eased away, heading for the coast.

'I can't thank you enough,' Bert said. The crisis over, his legs were shaking.

'Don't *ever* travel on your own out in the wilds. Especially in this border country, north of Spain. And don't ever, *ever* stop for any car that isn't clearly police. This is van muggers' territory. They prey on solitary vans. They're after your wallet, credit cards, cameras, laptops — anything they can sell in the back streets of places like Marseilles.'

'I didn't know,' said Bert.

'It's not the sort of thing you'll find in tourist brochures. I'm Terry. This is Bob

— his missus is still in their van. My missus died, a couple of years ago. We're heading south together. You'd better join us, make a convoy.'

'Thanks. I'm Bert, and this is Mary.'

'Hi,' said Mary. 'I've got the kettle on. Do you boys fancy a cup of tea?'

'I'll fetch the missus,' Bob said. 'Is there room for us all inside?'

'I'll make room — if I have to sit on the roof,' said Mary.

★   ★   ★

Twenty minutes too early for her appointment, Kelly waited nervously in her father's car. This was where abstract strategy had to be turned into sweaty fact, with nobody there to do it but herself. A blast of wind hit the car and rain spattered against the windows. Scottish autumn came wetter than in Italy. She checked her watch.

Had she remembered everything? She twisted round. A case of Sophie's wine was sitting in the back seat, for easy lifting. She felt her pocket: the waiter's friend — cork remover — was neatly in its place. She grinned as she remembered her grand-father's instructions over his mobile last night, from somewhere on the Spanish border: 'Open half-a-dozen

134

bottles, until you can do it like a professional, then pour the lot down the sink, not your throat.'

Would it work, this test marketing? The restaurant owner had agreed to see her — but what if he only took one sip, then threw her out?

She swallowed nervously. If disaster struck, she would have to find another Italian restaurant, then another, until she had fulfilled her part of the deal and done what she had promised when everybody was sitting around the kitchen table.

Had Dieter and Sophie managed to persuade the bank to cover the cost of Paulo's help? Would the restaurant owner be prepared to pay her anything like the price she had calculated, having checked out his wine list, and guessed at the huge margin he'd be charging?

Her mind jittered nervously back and forwards. What was Dieter doing? She really liked the big German and his silences, sensing way-above-normal sensitivity for any man. But she was wasting her time there. Anybody could see that he had eyes only for Sophie. Even if she was a lot older than he was.

Not that she herself had *that* kind of interest in him. But he'd been nice.

Kelly checked her watch. Sophie was a

warm, attractive woman. Had grown and blossomed over the harvest crisis and shown real courage. Kelly liked her too and wished her well, but was a little jealous.

What about her father? Was he caught in the same magnet-pull that had drawn in Dieter. What was it about red hair that attracted men? She ran fingers through her own dark hair, then urgently checked the mirror.

So what if her father was attracted to the woman? That was good. A sign that he had finally put her mother's death behind him, and was moving on. Whatever it was, he seemed happy and relaxed. Whether it was the challenges of sorting out the wine and the vineyard's finances, or something a whole lot more personal, he was more like the father she had always known. Not the quiet, introverted recluse he had become. Anything was better than that . . .

Kelly glanced down at her watch again and gulped. Getting out of the car, she opened the rear door and dragged the case of wine towards her. It weighed a ton. Balancing it on her hip, she closed the door and remote-locked the car.

Where were the words she had carefully written last night to be her opening sales pitch? They had vanished completely from her mind. She stood, blinking, in the driving rain. Yes, that was the first sentence, more or less. It sounded stilted, feeble. Maybe she should make up something else. Or simply leave it to chance and hope that better words would come when they were needed.

Gathering her courage, she walked towards the restaurant door.

Then past it. Her heart was thundering and her legs shaking, as her resolve simply evaporated. She walked on, her face crimson, in the rain. It was fifty metres beyond the restaurant before she could stop her mindless bolting.

This was stupid. Craven. Other people were depending on her. If she failed without trying, then a small vineyard would collapse, a red-haired woman's dream would finally implode and out of all their efforts would come only bankruptcy.

Kelly gritted her teeth. She was a graduate in Business. Marketing had been her specialist subject. In the eyes of the world, she was an expert. A professional.

Was she a woman or a mouse? Kelly turned, and checked. She hadn't grown a tail. Not yet. Her jaw firmed and she frowned. She could do this thing, must do it. Grimly, she turned and retraced her steps towards the restaurant door.

Pushing it open with her shoulder, she stepped inside.

6

One morning everyone wakened to find autumn gone. Winter had arrived without a word of warning. Grey skies drained the colour from the valley, and woodsmoke filled the air. On most days, there were snow flurries in the wind. It was bitterly cold.

A visit to Alba's street market was needed to buy David winter clothing. From the passenger seat of Sophie's battered old Fiat, he watched the valley's vineyards flow past his window. The beautiful russets and yellows of only weeks before were now dull bronze and black, accentuating the stark geometric patterns of the vine trellises set across every slope in the valley.

There wasn't a soul to be seen. Everybody would be working in the cellars now like himself, keeping the wine company, as Sergio put it, and fielding Paulo as he dropped in, taking samples for his lab.

David smiled: it was strange how the results were always brought back at night, just in time for Paulo to be invited to stay for dinner, thus defeating his wifely-imposed diet once again. But the kitchen door was never closed and locals often drifted in for a cup of tea or coffee in the passing, gathering Sophie into the valley culture once again.

'I love this place,' he said quietly. 'It's timeless. Beautiful.'

'I'm glad,' she replied.

It was somehow important that this quiet man should share her instinctive love of the valley and its people, the start of the obsession which had driven her to bring her family here to rescue a failing marriage, to find a new way forward out of the moneyed but sterile boredom which was destroying them. But you couldn't reinvent the electricity which once had come so naturally. It was a desperate gamble and it had failed, leaving her to face the problems on her own.

Yet it had left her also on the cusp of a new chapter in her life, to reinvent herself, find new courage and self-confidence. The extended family that the Old Ones had gathered around her had transformed everything. They had made her fight their own and had come up with a whole new strategy to get the vineyard back on its feet. For these last few weeks she had felt new life and hope flow through her.

She cut down from the valley road to the outskirts of the old red-roofed town, set among the dark trees of its river's woodlands, then swung into a quiet side street, and parked. 'We'll walk from here,' she said practically. 'When it's market day in Alba, people come from miles around. It's the biggest of the local markets.'

'So long as it sells thick, warm jackets,' David said. He smiled wryly. 'I didn't pack, or plan, to stay this long.'

Sophie laughed. 'You're here for as long as it takes, like Dieter. It's an open prison. I'm keeping you until you're not needed any more — or until you walk away.'

Open prisons have their own invisible chains. She had staked everything on his advice, and he couldn't leave until she was in safer waters. However, David was an honest man: there was another reason too. He didn't *want* to walk away. Nor did he want to pause and analyse his feelings. It was enough to live each day as it came and enjoy its magic.

They followed the stream of people down to the old cathedral and the heart of the town. 'I thought the bank would have advanced you more than they did,' he said, changing the subject.

Sophie grimaced. 'It was barely enough to convert a couple of rooms.'

'Maybe not a bad thing. It lets you test the market. See if you and Maria can cope before you turn the whole villa upside down.'

'True. It could as easily have been nothing at all. Dieter being there, and negotiating, swung the deal. A woman on her own has no chance here — it's a man's world, in these wine valleys.'

'He's a man of many talents,' David said. 'Beneath that silent exterior, he can turn his hand to anything.'

'His plumbing and plastering work are as good as any tradesman's.'

'And he's cheaper too,' David teased. 'He's doing it for free — simply to have the chance to stay on and make you smile.'

Sophie coloured. 'He's so young,' she said.

'And you're so old . . . ' David ducked as she flicked a hand at him. 'Just think, you could go down in history. Like Helen of Troy, whose face launched a thousand ships, Sophie of Alba, whose face launched a thousand *en suites* . . . '

Sophie laughed outright. David and Dieter were good for her. They made an easy-going team, comfortable in each other's company, with laughter never far away. 'Conversion work doesn't have the same ring to it,' she complained.

'Let history judge that.' David peered past the cathedral to the busy square beyond, a riot of colour from the different stall awnings. 'Is that a clothes stall over there?' he asked.

'Yes, but don't rush in. There are hundreds of stalls, right through to the far side of town. Have a good look round. See what's on offer. And always remember that stallholders *expect* you to bargain them down — it's part of their culture. Play one off against the other.'

'Sure,' said David absently. 'Hey! Look at these jeans — they're half the price you'd pay for this quality back home. And these work shirts — '

'You're here for a work jacket,' she reminded him.

'Uh-huh.' David picked up two pairs of jeans and a couple of thick winter shirts, then caught the stallholder's eye and pointed to the white Fiat van drawn up behind: the unisex changing room for any street market. The stallholder nodded. 'Back in a minute,' David said, stepping up inside the rear doors, and closing them.

'A good man that one. Not afraid of work.'

Sophie turned. It was Maria, down to raid the food stalls, but happy to spend the day searching through clothes she had no intention of buying. 'He's looking for a jacket,' Sophie said. 'Watch him. He'll buy everything he's taken into that van and pay double what he should.'

'He needs a wife.'

The brown eyes which were so dark they

were almost black, twinkled.

'No,' said Sophie firmly. 'It is not like that.'

'Of course not,' said Maria solemnly. 'At least he doesn't make sheep's eyes at you like the young one does.'

'I'm old enough to be Dieter's mother.'

'Absolutely,' said Maria. She tilted her head, an ancient sparrow, listening for a worm. Or anything.

'Maria! Stop it,' Sophie said crossly.

The dark wrinkled face assumed an expression of total innocence.

'Stop what? I am standing here in place of *your* mother. It is therefore my duty to find you a better man than the one you rightly sent away.'

'They are friends. Helping me. Dieter with the conversion work, and David working with Sergio and Paulo to get the wine through the DOC tests. That's all . . . '

'Exactly what I've been telling the other valley women.'

'Dieter is far too young; David thinks only of sorting out the vineyard.'

Maria nodded. 'It's the man's responsibility. Sara likes him.'

'He spoils her silly. I could barely get her to go back to school. She spent a week beneath every sick tractor and every old car and APE van in the valley.'

Maria nodded. 'Sara was made for here. And the men like David. He knows our customs. Says 'thank you for help' by doing things, like working on people's cars and tractors. A good man, a natural father. If you were my own daughter — '

'No,' said Sophie firmly. 'Here he comes. Look at him. He's *wearing* that work-shirt and the jeans, with his own stuff crammed into that old plastic bag. That's no way to argue down prices, with the labels hanging from him . . . '

Maria tutted sympathetically. 'He needs a wife to look after him,' she said.

★ ★ ★

That did it. With one failed marriage behind her, Sophie wasn't ready to enter another relationship. She was happy to operate with men as equals, friends, but not on any other level. David understood this. It was Dieter who was the problem. He must be told that his infatuation should stop. And quickly.

That afternoon, she climbed to where Dieter was working in the east wing bedrooms. He looked up and smiled, a smear of plaster across his nose. She fought the urge to reach down, and wipe it off.

'Dieter, we must talk,' she started briskly.

The giant German rolled smoothly from the floor to his feet. 'I'll get David,' he said. 'Is he out in the cellars?'

'Not David. Just you and me.'

'Oh.' His eyes studied her. 'I think I shall not enjoy this talk.'

'Don't be silly. I just want to set things straight between us. I know you have . . . an affection . . . for me. Which is very flattering. You are such a nice man, that the last thing I want is to hurt your feelings. But, Dieter, I'm not ready to become involved with anybody again. And I'm too old for you. You're so young — '

'Not true,' Dieter said quietly. 'Because of things I have seen, some days I feel a thousand years old.' The big head drooped, eye contact broken. Sophie waited, but there was no explanation. Only the usual defensive silence.

'I am not the woman you are searching for,' she said simply.

'Then who is this woman?'

'Only you will know her, when you find her.'

Dieter absently smeared more wet plaster across his nose. 'And how shall I know her?' he asked bleakly.

Sophie stood on tiptoe, wiping the smears from his face. 'You will know, because that day you will no longer stop in the middle of sentences about yourself,' she smiled. 'You will know, when you simply tell her what is hurting you so badly inside. When you find yourself telling that to any woman, you will know that she — and only she — is the woman you are looking for.'

★   ★   ★

'Somebody should at least have sent me a birthday card,' Mary grumbled.

'Why? You wanted to be a gypsy. Follow the sun.' Bert glanced over from his chair in the Spanish sunshine, a four-day-old newspaper in his hands — and an English one at that, without a line of news on Scottish football. 'The downside is that nobody knows where gypsies are going to be. So nobody sends a card.'

'They could have phoned. Asked us for the site's address.'

'We change sites every couple of weeks. On a whim. At random.'

'It's not fair,' she said stubbornly. 'Kelly should have sent me a card.'

'After that row at Sophie's when she tried to stop you leaving there?'

'Wasn't a row. We had different opinions, that's all.'

Mary watched Bert disappear beneath his elderly newspaper, which had already toured the ex-pat British colony. Terry and Bob were right: there were more Brits here than back in England, she thought glumly. You met, talked for hours, ate and drank more than was good for you. Got tired of the same routine and the same company and pushed on to the next site south — only to find that half the colony had moved there already, to escape you. Welcome back. While the sun just shone, every day, taking the guesswork out of the weather. Boring.

'Bert?' she said.

'Uhuh?'

'What are we doing tonight? To celebrate?'

Bert glanced across. 'Your birthday, so it's your choice,' he said. 'We can heat up a chicken tandoori from the supermarket, or walk down to one of the cafés on the front.'

'How about a hotel?'

'Can't afford a hotel.'

'Don't be mean.'

'I'm not mean, just realistic. Think of how much we spent on diesel getting here.' Noisily, he turned a page and settled down, trying not to let her see his face, because she could read him like an open book. And behind that shifty face, there was a secret. It was his job to keep her here while half the campsite scuttled around out of view, finishing preparations for her birthday party.

Mary picked up a handful of sandy grit from the side of her chair. Took aim.

It scattered like shrapnel across his page. 'Hey!' he complained. 'You've made Ronaldo go down, holding his ankle!'

'You're mean,' she said. 'I should have listened to my dad. He said you were only a wee chancer from the worst council scheme in Edinburgh.'

'And I should have listened to my mother,' Bert replied. 'She told me you were nothing but stocking seams and lipstick. She said you'd spend every penny I had, then run away.'

Mary snorted. 'So I would,' she said, 'if I could only get at them.'

'Look after your pennies and they'll look after you,' Bert said virtuously.

A fresh burst of shrapnel exploded across his newspaper.

He sighed. 'OK. I'll go and ask at the site office if there's any mail come in.'

★   ★   ★

'What's up with Dieter?' David asked. 'I saw him striding up the valley road.'

148

'He wanted a break,' Sophie answered evasively.

David studied her. The silence lengthened. 'Paulo phoned,' he said. 'He's got the results of the latest tests. They're good. But he's coming tonight to talk us through what we still need to do.'

'Then I'd better start cooking,' Sophie sighed.

'What's up?' he asked directly. 'There's something wrong.'

'Dieter. It's my fault.' Sophie took a deep breath. 'I told him that I was getting embarrassed by his infatuation — ' She broke off, at David's face. 'Not like that, of course; as gently as I could.'

The phone rang. Sophie ignored it.

'There's no such thing as gentle for something like that,' David murmured.

'I wish I hadn't done it now. *Si?*'

Sophie picked up the phone, listened, then held it wordlessly to David.

'My mother?'

Sophie shook her head, covering the mouthpiece. 'It's Kelly. I'm scared . . . there's so much . . . everything . . . depending on this call. You take it. Please.'

'Hi, Kelly,' David said. 'What's the news? How are you?'

'Fine. What's up with Sophie? I was trying to tell her — '

'How did you get on with the wine?'

He sensed a smile, and relief engulfed him.

'Oh, I did as you said,' she told him airily. 'Carted it round half-a-dozen Italian restaurants.'

'And?'

'And sold everything but the last half-dozen crates.'

'She's sold the wine!' he shouted to Sophie.

'Ouch! Warn me next time you're going to bellow! Now, why don't you ask me what I did with the last half-dozen crates?' Kelly's young voice sounded as if she was in the room, brimming with laughter and confidence.

'Consider yourself asked,' David said weakly.

'I took them to one of the big supermarkets,' said Kelly airily. 'Got an appointment with the boss guy, and asked if he would like a glass of wine. He warned me that he was a wine buff. I said: all the better. I opened a bottle for him and produced the glass I'd spent twenty minutes shining up before — '

'And . . . ?' prompted David impatiently.

'He sniffed the cork, then the bottle. Held the glass to the light. Swirled it round and swigged. Sloshed it round his mouth — disgusting. Did everything but gargle with it. Then swallowed, smacked his lips, and

150

went through it all again.'

'Put us out our misery,' beseeched David. 'What did he say?'

'He asked how much. I told him. He knocked off £1.50 a bottle, then smiled like a shark. What he doesn't know, is that he's still paying more than the restaurants. He's willing to do £2.75 a bottle, if you can fill his order.'

'Which is?'

'A thousand crates — that's twelve thousand bottles,' Kelly said calmly.

David leaned against the wall. 'She's gone and sold another twelve thousand bottles,' he said weakly. 'That's — ' His mind refused to work.

'It's thirty-three thousand pounds,' Kelly supplied the answer. 'About forty thousand in total.'

'You've just won the lottery,' David told Sophie.

'Not all profit,' Kelly warned. 'There will be shipping costs, cleaning, labelling and packing charges. But it should make these Italian bankers take notice.'

Sophie grabbed the phone from David's limp hand. 'Sophie here. Did you say twelve thousand bottles?'

'Have you that much in stock.'

'With about eight thousand bottles to spare.'

'Good,' said Kelly. 'In fact, excellent.'

'Why?' asked Sophie.

'If one supermarket's keen, why not try another?'

From ruin, this giant leap towards solvency. By selling that first vintage, she could pay off interest on her debts, and some of the capital sum too. So long as she kept enough back as working capital to fund herself through the year ahead.

Sophie's mind raced. 'Commission,' she said.

'Whose?'

'Yours. For acting as my selling agent.'

'No, Sophie. I couldn't possibly. I was only helping out.'

'You did better than any professional. I'll ask Guiseppe, he'll know the usual rates. This is a proper business deal, or nothing, Kelly.'

A long silence, on the phone.

'Have you a job?' Sophie asked directly.

'Well, no. I was taking a year out . . .'

'Then you have a job right now. Selling my wine. Maybe even working with Guiseppe to try and sell some of the co-operativa's wines. From small vineyards that have been worked by families for centuries. The big wines, like Barolo and Barbaresco, are marketed in America. The rest of us are small-scale producers, selling mostly to touring Germans and Scandanavians. If you can open up a new British market for us — '

'Gosh,' said Kelly.

'Whatever else, you have saved the vineyard with that single order. Turned dusty bottles into solid gold.'

'I'm glad,' said Kelly simply.

She hesitated, over a thousand miles away.

'How is Dieter?' she finally asked. 'How's the conversion work getting on?'

* * *

'We should be going to a hotel,' Mary sulked.

'Waste of money,' said Bert.

She clutched his arm to steady herself, as they walked through the scented purple dusk of the path down to the town. The night throbbed with the shrill noise of cicadas. 'These grasshopper things — ' she started.

Bert waited, then asked, 'What about them.'

'Have they got to make a din like that?'

'So would you if you were left outside every night.'

Mary stumbled on a cobblestone as they headed down through the small town towards the sea. She gripped his arm more tightly. 'Where are we going?'

'I booked a table at your favourite harbour café.'

Mary gritted her teeth. Of course she liked that café, sitting in the shade and watching fishermen working on their boats in the hot sun outside. But that was for lazy coffee. She couldn't believe he was being so mean. Yes, money was tight, given their carefully planned monthly budget. But surely the time for belt-tightening was later? Not now, when she felt so many miles away from home, missing her family, getting older, and wanting somebody to make a special fuss of her.

They came out into the harbour square, deserted in the early dark. It was too soon for the Spanish to start eating, so only a few of the cafés had lights on, with bored waiters standing outside. Anything was better than dusting the tables, Mary thought bitterly.

'Well,' she said, 'that's blown your plan out the water.'

Bert stopped short. 'What has?'

'Our café is closed. Got no lights on.'

Bert stared, stricken. What could possibly have gone wrong?

'Maybe it wasn't worth their while, opening up for only the two of us? Maybe they've gone up to the supermarket for that last chicken tandoori?'

Bert fought panic. He'd done his part of the job. Where was everybody?

'So what's our Plan B?' she asked sweetly. 'Head for a fancy hotel, with both of us wearing jeans? Or race them for that chicken tandoori you were promising, and maybe even buy a packet of crisps to go with it for my birthday treat?'

Bert cleared his throat. 'Very funny. Let's take a walk round the harbour and sniff the air that smells of Africa while I try to think up a Plan B.'

'Sounds good. But I'm starving.'

'That makes two of us.'

'Let's try another café,' she suggested, relenting. He was clearly shocked to find his planned night in ruins.

'Wouldn't be the same,' Bert argued. 'Let's walk round the harbour.'

'We walked round it this morning. They haven't made any changes since.'

'I'll think of something.'

'I already have. We're going to another café.'

'Not just yet. I'm not hungry.'

'You've just said you were.'

'Did I? Don't remember.'

'Bert,' she said firmly, 'there are times when you need a good woman to pick you up and tell you what to do. Come on. I'm taking you for a meal.'

He looked back desperately, but Mary

hauled him ruthlessly forward. They had barely walked fifty yards, when a band struck up behind them. A small but enthusiastic band. Playing something that, on a good day, with a following wind, might just have been *Happy birthday to you.*

Somebody with a radio and a sick sense of humour? Mary spun round. The deserted café was ablaze with light. Lights inside, around its patio, fairy lights on every tree. Even the *cicadas* stilled, taken aback. A motley collection of German, Dutch, Swedish and British campers were sitting around every table, or standing beside the red-faced and furiously blowing band, beckoning her back to the one empty table, at the edge of the light, where candle flames flickered in the purple dark.

'Happy birthday, lassie,' said Bert, his legs almost giving out in relief.

He leaned down and kissed her astonished face, to the applause of half the campsite — who were up for any party, so long as it involved food and booze.

'But . . . ' Mary spluttered, 'nobody was here, half a minute ago.'

'I know,' said Bert. 'I'll kill whoever thought of that twist to our surprise.'

★ ★ ★

Hours later, back in the dark and quiet of their campervan, he felt her stir. 'Still awake?' he asked. 'Have you eaten too much? Are you OK?'

She wriggled closer. 'I'm fine,' she said.

He twisted round, placing his arm across her shoulders.

'Enjoy your party?' he asked.

'It was lovely. Such a surprise.'

'Too right about that,' said Bert, with feeling.

Silence, then she stirred again. 'Bert?'

'Whazzat?' He struggled back from the edge of sleep.

'Know what would have made everything perfect?'

'Mmm?'

'If David and Kelly had come. And Dieter, that big German. Sophie too.'

'But they're thousands of miles away.'

'I miss them. They make me want to go home.'

Bert's heart sank. 'We have no home. This van is our home.'

'I know that,' she said impatiently. 'And I love it. But I wish . . . if only we could meet up, see them all again, before Christmas. Just for a few days. I know it's weeks of driving, but it would be so nice to be together, as family again.'

In the dark, Bert swallowed. 'OK, I'll phone David. See if we can go back there — catch a train, a bus, whatever. Have a few days' holiday in Alba. Then come back here. It can be your Christmas present.'

There were times when you thought you knew every nook and cranny of a man — yet he could still turn round and surprise you.

'Mary's eyes filled. 'Could we do that? Honestly?'

'I'll try. That's all I'm promising.'

'Bert, you're wonderful.'

'I know,' he said modestly.

'Just don't let it go to your head. Don't say another word and ruin it.'

'What if we — ?'

'Shoosh!' said Mary. She snuggled in.

           ★ ★ ★

'Well? Are you warmer, working, now?'

David looked up from sweeping the cellar floor to find Sophie had slipped around the cellar door and closed it behind her against the bitingly cold wind. 'It's always warm in here,' he replied. 'Even when I'm not sweeping out.'

The warmth came from the fermenting wine, although, as the fermentation slowed, both waste gases and temperature tended to drop, no longer compensating for the bitter cold outside. He was glad to be wearing thicker shirts and jeans.

Sophie looked at the rows of working vats. 'It won't be long until we throw open the cellar doors to let the winter in,' she said. 'That's how the valley people have killed off the yeast and stopped fermentation for centuries.'

'A couple of weeks yet, Paulo says.' David leaned on his brush.

'And he's sure the wine will pass, this time round?'

'In terms of what he calls 'the numbers', you are almost there already. It's only the final taste of the raw young wine he can't really control. But I saw him take a sip and swill it round his mouth, then spit it out, and nod. He's saved the vintage for you. In ten months' time, there will be more new bottles for Kelly to sell — and this time, it will be high quality *Nebbiolo D'Alba*, not only table wine.'

'I can't believe our luck has turned,' Sophie said quietly. 'I've had so little good fortune, I keep expecting some new disaster to come and destroy everything.'

'Why should it? Where's Dieter?'

'Gone early to bed.' Sophie winced. 'I feel so bad about him. He's turned quiet again.

Hurting and withdrawn. I'm scared that trying to stop his infatuation might have cost me his friendship too.'

'No chance of that,' said David.

'But what if it was all based on what he thought was love?'

'Unlikely. But even if it was, lots of love affairs stay on as lifelong friendships.'

'Who told you that?'

'History, for one thing. It's a like a book on car mechanics — only it tells you what makes people tick. It shows how ancient people lived their lives, how they strayed, how they loved and lost. It's all there, everything that we read about in today's tabloids. They were ordinary people too, not just giant figures. And people never change, we're still the same. Blundering into the same mistakes, then making the same heroic recoveries.'

When she got him talking about his subject, she could see how he brought everything to life: what an excellent lecturer he was. She sighed. In another time, and another set of circumstances, she could find herself drifting down the well-trodden path with this man. Maria's hands were nudging her forward, but she wasn't ready, didn't want to risk the priceless friendship he had given her; the new self-respect, as well as the healthier vineyard.

'Sara just phoned,' she said abruptly. Then held up a hand as he threw the brush aside and headed for the door. 'Too late. She's gone. The phone was taken out of her hand by Hannah. She was more interested in finding out what would be on offer here at Christmas, so that she could make her own plans . . . '

Times had changed, David thought wryly. Kids today had far more licence than Kelly had ever been given. Brought into not only the central focus of the family, but given their own decision rights like any adult. Good, but dangerous too. What if they lacked the experience to make their decisions sensibly?

Her family: not his business. 'Are you bringing them both over for Christmas?' he asked. 'The money from the wine should be in by then.'

'Sara will be here whatever happens. What Hannah does will depend on what her father has to offer. Or her jet-set friends.'

David stayed quiet on that one too. 'What did Sara want?' he asked.

'She was full of questions about the wine . . . the tractors that you mended between you . . . what the valley men were doing . . . would you still be here by Christmas. Each of my daughters is chasing after someone who isn't me.'

She meant it as a joke, but her raw hurt showed.

'Not true,' said David gently. 'Sara loves this place and the valley people. But if you added that all together, it would still fall short of the love she has for you.'

Sophie blinked. This man could see her fears, and find the right words to calm them every time. He was far more dangerous, in his own quiet way, than Dieter. When a marriage failed, it was so easy to blunder towards someone who is the opposite of what the other partner had been. Over-compensating.

'Why don't you phone her back?' asked David.

'Who?'

'Sara. If she phoned you, it was to have a chat. And she would be talking about the minor things, before she got round to the things — and the people — who really matter. Kids are all the same.'

'How do you know?' she asked.

'Because I have spent my whole life teaching them. You have to be patient, let them get round to the difficult bit in their own way, and in their own time. Because it's only then that they will let you help them.'

He picked up the brush again, dark hair falling over a sombre face, where the calm clear eyes spoke of depth and understanding.

Still waters run deep, her mother had always said. Where Brian had been brilliant, extrovert, commanding: her mother had a saying for that one too — empty barrels make the most noise. Brian had proved empty, beneath his veneer of brilliance. This man had brought strength, calmness, and ideas which had turned the vineyard around. It was good to have him there, to lean on. Dangerous too, because liking could so easily slide into something else. Something stronger.

'OK,' she said. 'Let's phone the school again. What are you doing?'

'Finishing off the floor.'

'No, you're not. You're coming inside with me.' Sophie sighed. 'I need someone there to answer all her questions about vineyards and tractors, while she works through all the less important stuff — and gets round to me.'

The quiet face smiled as if it had been lit up from within.

'OK,' he said. 'Let's go.'

7

Sophie blew red hair from her face impatiently. No time to pin it back again while she was baking and planning how to fit everyone in over the Christmas holiday.

She paused, leaning on floury fists. Maria was already cleaning upstairs, where plaster dust had drifted into every nook and cranny. No question of using the newly converted rooms — their walls were still too damp. Even so, she would manage with a room to spare: two bedrooms for the girls; the big guest room for Bert and Mary again; the small bedroom with the view down the valley for Kelly. No need to disturb her own room, or David's . . . or Dieter's den, into which he seemed to have retired since they suspended his conversion work.

With all her heart, she wished she had never spoken so firmly to him.

Leave him be, David had said, he'll come round in his own time. She glanced at the clock: he would be pottering around the cellars, when he should be getting ready to drive up to Turin Airport and pick up the girls. Hannah had decided to come at the very last minute. A more exciting holiday with one of her posh school friends must have collapsed.

Sophie busied herself guiltily. She should be collecting them herself, but there were a million and one things still to do. Everything should be fine: David and Sara were thick as thieves. It was Hannah who was the problem — but even she would surely behave on the trip home from the airport.

Maybe David could work another miracle: but miracles and Hannah didn't belong in the same sentence. She was her father's daughter, with the same sharp, brilliant mind. Everything came too quick and easy to her — then the devil found work for her idle hands to do.

The kitchen door opened and Maria came in. 'Those big German feet of his,' she grumbled. 'They have carried plaster dust into every corner of the house. Do you want a cup of coffee? His dust has made me thirsty.'

'No time,' said Sophie. 'Too much to do before the girls arrive.'

'Take time. The girls and Kelly can hang the decorations. Make themselves useful. When I was their age . . . '

'I can almost remember being their age,' sighed Sophie. 'The whole world at my feet, and anything possible.'

'It is better to look back,' said Maria.

'You sound like an ancient grandmother,' Sophie laughed.

'I am an ancient grandmother. And content, for the first time in my life.'

Sophie wiped the worst of the flour off her hands onto her apron. 'I hope I've baked enough,' she sighed. 'So many people . . . it's so long since I had a houseful like this descending onto me.'

'This old house was made to be full. It is a family house.'

But never with such a strange mix of families, Sophie thought wryly. She should be nervous about everyone getting on. Somehow, she wasn't. Things would work out — even with Hannah.

From outside came the whine of a car being driven to the limit. A squeal of tyres, as it banked rather than turned in through her gate. Then the grate and slither of locked tyres on her courtyard.

'Not the girls?' Sophie exclaimed, stricken.

She raced to the door to see a local taxi sitting amid a cloud of burning rubber. The rear door opened and Bert emerged, shakily. He looked around the courtyard, caught her eye and waved.

'Does he always drive like that?' he asked weakly.

Mary crawled out behind. 'I'm definitely

166

walking next time.'

Sophie ran over, hugged her. 'Did you have a good trip?'

'Not a single problem,' Mary said.

'Apart from you dragging me onto the wrong platform.' Bert fished in the boot for their cases, while the driver continued to argue into his mobile phone.

'Well, you were standing in a trance.'

'I was thinking. Trying to see a proper sign in English.'

'In France? Why should they help the English?'

'True.' Bert drew out his wallet and began to search through the paper money. A sunburned hand reached over his shoulder, picked the euro note with the largest denomination.

'*Ciao,*' said the driver. His door slammed. Wheels spun. Still talking down his mobile phone, the car was screamed into a U-turn, which became a three-point turn, which launched him like an arrow through the gates.

Silence returned. Bert contentedly sniffed the woodsmoke-tinged mist which filled the valley. 'It's good to be home,' he said. 'I could murder a cup of tea.'

'Which means thank you very much for inviting us, Sophie,' Mary sighed. 'It's taken me nearly fifty years to get him to wipe his

167

feet. Teaching him manners has defeated me.'

'It would be easier, catching sunshine in a jar,' David said.

'Where were you?' his mother asked.

'In the cellars.'

'He lives in there,' complained Sophie.

'Maybe you could get him to adopt his dad,' Mary suggested.

★ ★ ★

Sophie was sitting in the kitchen with Bert and Mary when the phone rang. She excused herself and went through to the hall. '*Si?*' she asked.

'Sophie? How are you?'

She reached for the hallstand to steady herself.

'Brian? Is there a problem? The girls?'

'Relax. I ran them to the airport. They've just taken off. Thought I'd give you a bell, and see how you were doing before you set out to Turin to pick them up.'

What did he want? In a marriage that had known more downs than ups, Sophie had learned that a relaxed and considerate Brian generally had some nasty surprises which he was waiting for the right moment to spring on her.

'Everything's fine,' she said. Trying to sound relaxed.

'Sara says you've managed to sell some wine. Things are on the up.'

'So far, so good,' she said guardedly.

'And this year's vintage?'

'We're waiting for the tasting panel's verdict in the New Year.'

'You got some lab rat to put it right for you, I understand.'

Lab rat? Sophie fought down anger. Paulo was a friend. His bio-chemistry skills had nursed them through the DOC sampling tests, made the impossible, possible. 'We dealt with the problem professionally,' she said eventually.

More than Brian had done the year before.

'Good-oh. Are you having people staying for Christmas?'

The old sick feeling came flooding back at Brian's well-remembered trick of changing the focus of his attack, keeping her off-balance and floundering. How much had the girls told him? More correctly, how much had Sara told Hannah, and Hannah reported back to her father?

'A few,' she said. 'My friends.'

'Have you room for one more little one?'

Sophie's heart lurched. On the face of it, a friendly overture: OK, so the marriage has failed, but let's stay friends for the kids' sake. But Brian was a wheeler-dealer, incapable of any action that could be taken at face value. Did she want him to come over? To spend Christmas on edge, while he tried to manipulate her into whatever scheme he had in mind?

Once she would have jumped at the chance, hoping for reconciliation.

'Is that wise?' She forced herself to sound urbane. Controlled.

'It's old history. We both said — and did — things we would rather forget. But Christmas is for families. And New Year is the start of another calendar. A clean slate . . . '

Once she would have felt weak with relief, and hope.

'Come on,' Brian urged gently. 'Fair's fair. I was hoping to have the kids this Christmas. I was going to invite you over, to have Christmas together at my flat — there's plenty of rooms for everybody. I thought we could try, for a few days, to live in peace and give the girls a good time.'

He paused. 'Now you're having them over in Italy, I'm on my own. Lonely.'

Somewhere deep in Sophie, something stirred. Pity? Some residual scrap of love for the man, which had never died? It had not always been rows and coldness: once, the chemistry had been pretty good.

'Don't make me beg,' Brian said.

There was that final room to spare. Sophie drew a ragged breath. She was about to invite him over, when an older and harder Sophie stepped firmly in. The script was too perfect. The words too much what he thought she'd be longing to hear, offering a chance to reinvent the marriage. All debts and anger cancelled out.

'You should have mentioned it sooner,' she said quietly.

'Me? I'm a creature of impulse. Remember?'

The tone was light, confident. A man sure of victory. Saying the right words so flawlessly that it had to be an act. There was a sub-plot in this somewhere, but she was too weighed-down with emotional baggage to see it.

'I'm sorry,' she said. 'Truly. But part of the villa is closed for conversion. I don't have a room to spare, Brian. If you had phoned sooner, I might have invited fewer friends. I don't know. But the day before Christmas Eve is far too late to return as the prodigal husband. Sorry.'

'Not even for old times' sake?'

'Maybe you're thinking of other old times. The ones I remember finished in a divorce court. If you want to explore the possibility of another start, pick a better time. I'm busy. Run off my feet.'

'OK, old girl,' he said. 'But should you change your mind . . . '

Too sweet. Too reasonable. There was a hidden agenda.

'You'll be the first to know,' she said levelly.

'I'll settle for that. Merry Christmas, Soph.'

'Merry Christmas, Brian.'

'Unlikely, if I have to spend it on my own . . . ' He let the words hang.

Then, just as she was about to speak, he cut her off.

★ ★ ★

Kneeling on the cellar roof, David hammered home the last few nails. This was a winter chore he had been postponing. But now that the cellar doors had been thrown open to the winter, so that its cold would kill the yeast in the wine, and stop fermentation naturally, its turn had come.

Over the years, rioting creeper had done its worst, burrowing up and under the pantiles. It had cracked the odd tile here and there, leaving space for wind-driven rain to explore, rotting the wooden planking under the tiles.

He had borrowed a few pantiles from Sergio and wood from one of the other growers down the valley. Part of the give-and-take of valley life, where you did what was needed for your neighbour, then asked what you needed in return. He felt at ease with the informal barter system. It was an ancient, and better, culture.

The creeper had been cut back, and the replacement wood fitted. Now all he had to do was re-hang the tiles. David laid his hammer aside, and savoured the scent of woodsmoke that was everywhere. From the grey space beyond the cedars, birds called. Peace: the whole valley and this house were steeped in it.

The ladder below him creaked. Sophie? Dieter?

Sara's face and bright eyes rose above the roof edge. 'What are you doing up here, David?' she demanded.

'Repairing the roof. The wood was rotten.' David reached for the first pantile in the neat stack at his side. Fitted its shoulder carefully over the gutter of the tile it now overlapped. He picked up his hammer, fished out a nail, and anchored the tile in place. Then repeated the exercise with another tile.

'So that's how it's done,' said Sara.

'Easy. You finish the row, then set the next row over it, to shed the rainwater down. Shoulders over edges. Tails over heads . . . ' To illustrate, he picked a loose tile and placed it over one of the tiles he had just anchored into place. 'Give water somewhere to run, and it will never trouble you,' he said.

Sara watched. 'Can I come up and do some of them?'

'What if you fall off?'

'You haven't.'

'What will your mother say?'

'I won't tell her if you don't.'

The cellar roof was low and its slope minimal. She'd be safe enough.

'OK. Take my hand.' David eased her onto the roof, and showed her how to use knees and feet to anchor herself there. 'It's like climbing a mountain,' he warned. 'Three points of contact . . . otherwise you'll slide, and I'll be in trouble.'

'I won't slide. Can I do the next tile, please?'

David handed the pantile over, and watched. She worked neatly and without fuss. Whatever her problems at school, with a brilliant father and younger sister to outshine her, she was a quick learner for practical work. Sergio and the valley men were right: this slip of a girl was born to work on a vineyard — shoulder to shoulder with the men, as Sophie had worked.

The pile of tiles diminished. 'How do we finish off?' Sara asked.

'I'll ease up the top row. Slip the new tiles under that.'

'No nails? Won't they just slide out?'

'The weight of the top tiles should anchor them.'

'I understand.' She finished the final row, and inspected the mended section of roof. 'Not bad,' she said. 'These new tiles are lighter in colour.'

'They'll weather down.'

She smiled. 'That's another job I can do.'

'You're making me redundant.'

'Never.'

'It's true.' David straightened, looking down over the grey contours of the valley, the endless vine trellises disappearing into the mist. 'I'll miss all this. But I've research work waiting to do. There's a university over in the States wondering where on earth I've got to. They'll be sending out a search party soon.'

Sara's eyes sparkled. 'You can hide. They'll never think of looking here.'

'They're Americans. They'll have blood-hounds. With wrinkled sad faces and long floppy ears. Bloodhounds always find their man. Then their bosses will drag me back to slavery in my research room.'

'We could disguise you as Sergio.'

'I'd hate that stubble.'

'Then we could disguise you as Maria.'

'I'd hate the wrinkled stockings.'

Sara laughed outright. 'Well, Mum and I

could come over in the dark. Bring lots of horses with us. Tie our lassoes to the window of your research room and drag it out. Then the three of us could gallop away to the Badlands and escape.'

'Who would look after your vines, then?'

Her smile faded, into a small frown. 'Don't go, David. Please.'

Another tie, he thought. Another invisible chain.

'Not for a bit, anyway,' he said. 'Come on. Let's get down.'

He slid onto the ladder, ready to steady her as she made the transition from the low roof. As he reached out to drop the hammer to the ground, and leave his right hand free, he felt it taken from him.

He glanced down. Hannah. 'I've got it,' she said. 'I was listening.'

David guided Sara's groping foot onto the safety of the ladder, then came down steadily. Sara followed slowly, face flushed bright red. As in the car from Turin, he watched her retreat deep into herself. Not the self he had come to recognize. Instead, the silent and insecure child he'd seen on that first visit before he found the key to let the other Sara out.

He reached for the hammer. 'Thanks,' he said.

Hannah watched him. The same direct

gaze he had caught every time he lifted his eyes to the rear mirror on that trip back from the airport. A very adult weighing-up gaze which never faltered, when she found his eyes on her. Thirteen-going-on-thirty, Sophie had once warned.

'I wouldn't plan on staying much longer,' she said eventually.

'Hannah!' Sara exclaimed. Her sister ignored her.

'So, start looking for an exit route from the niche you've made. As the indispensable adviser and right-hand man. The friend in need.'

David's hackles rose. This was no child. Here was the mind of an equal, incisive, logical. Ruthless. Her father's daughter, Sophie had said sadly. Sara is the one who takes after me. We're the idiots in the family.

'Simply a friend,' he answered finally. 'I stayed to help your mother get the wine passed by the DOC. After that, she won't need help. And I'll head off to my sabbatical research semester in America.'

'Good. There's nothing for you here.'

'Why should there be?'

'Why, indeed?' Hannah studied him, her light blue eyes alive with intelligence and self-confidence. 'Anything that needs to be done, can be done by my dad — he's coming

177

back, you know. They'll patch things over, make another start. We're going to be a family once again.'

This sounded like a planned invasion. 'Does your mother know this?'

Hannah shrugged. 'She soon will. She'll grab the chance. She's always needed him. He's the strong one in the partnership.'

'But there isn't a partnership any more,' said David, unable to believe that he was talking like this to any child. 'They're divorced. And since then, your mother has moved on. Learned to stand on her own two feet. Fight off bankruptcy, bring in a harvest. Finding strength she never knew she had before.'

He turned to pick up the ladder. Before he could lift it onto his shoulder, Sara was at the other end of it tacitly showing that she was on his side, but not up to arguing with her younger sister.

That angered him, more than anything else had done.

He turned back. 'Your mother is a different woman,' he said. 'Someone who's been tempered by fire into solid steel. She's no longer the weak one, the dependent one. In the future, she will make her own way through life. Her own choices, her own terms and conditions. And I think these will be pretty tough to live up to — for your father, or any other man in her life. So, if you've cooked up something between you, you'd better tell him this: the rules have changed; your mother isn't a pushover any more.'

'Bravo,' said Sara. She picked up her end of the ladder. 'Can you take me down to Alba, David? We can buy some roast chestnuts. Down in the arcade, where the Africans sell their jewellery from their blankets on the ground.'

'Roasted chestnuts?' said Hannah. 'Count me in!'

These were Sophie's girls. She expected him to be friendly, treat them both as equals. For Sara, he'd made the effort without a second's thought. For Hannah, he must make that effort too — this time, out of a sense of duty.

'OK,' David sighed. 'I'm finished here. Let's go.'

★ ★ ★

It was Christmas Eve. The whole valley lay still and silent beneath a sky which was ablaze with stars — no city lights to dim their brilliance. In the villa, Sophie and Sara were finishing the decorations. Hannah, legs folded beneath her, was curled in a chair apart from

179

the others, reading. Dieter was sitting quietly, at the edge of the group: he had scarcely spoken a word, all night.

The rest were too busy talking to notice.

'The idea is good. This marketing will help small producers,' Sergio said.

Guiseppe translated for Kelly. 'It's going well,' he murmured. 'But stress that you aren't tying up their main production.'

'I want to run this as an experiment,' Kelly said. 'Not as a major adjustment to everyone's way of working. Rather, trying to find a market for the wine they cannot sell at present. Gathering together a lot of small vineyard labels. Then presenting them as a regional brand — individual variations on the theme.'

'*La Co-operativa* will help,' Guiseppe threw his weight behind her. 'It's only an extension of what we're doing already in gathering grapes from small producers, then blending them into our own labelled wine. With Kelly's scheme, we can help small independent wineries too. We could hold their surplus wine, then act as a central warehouse for shipping out to Britain, once Kelly wins us orders. That would cut operational costs.'

Paulo leaned towards Sergio, translating quietly. Sergio nodded.

'The proposal is so simple, it has to work,' he declared.

Paulo frowned. 'Guiseppe, the big producers might complain if they see this co-operated action as a threat,' he warned.

'The big producers sell major wines like *Barolo* or *Barbaresco*. We're not competing there, internationally. We are selling lesser-known grapes and wines, in tiny quantities. Developing a new market niche, not gate-crashing their market.'

Kelly studied Dieter: sombre and silent. What had happened to him, she wondered. 'Dieter,' she said, 'this could be the job I've always wanted. Working with the small guys, selling their surplus wine. Small vineyards, that look just like Sophie's, and have been run traditionally by families from the start of time.'

Her dark hair shone like a crow's wings, he thought. The enthusiasm in her face and eyes brought the first smile to his face in days. He sensed that, somehow, she was wanting his goodwill, his benediction, almost.

'I agree with Sergio,' he said. 'I think it is an excellent idea.'

'Can you help me work out the contract details?' she asked.

Before Dieter could answer, Guiseppe stepped in.

'These are the wine valleys,' he said. 'No need for contracts. We will visit the valley people, one by one. I will explain what you are offering to them and act as translator for their questions. The men will listen, look at you, and judge. If they think you're honest and buy into the idea, then they'll shake your hand. That is a binding contract, here.'

'But Sophie says it is a man's culture. Men negotiate only with men.'

'I will be there,' said Guiseppe, smiling. 'Everybody knows me.'

Kelly looked across. Dieter read the mute appeal, in her eyes.

'I shall come too,' he said. 'If it's men they want to negotiate with, then you have two of them in your team.'

Kelly smiled. 'Back home, I would never stand for this,' she warned.

'When in Rome . . . ' smiled Guiseppe.

'Or even *Piemonte*,' Paulo added, helping himself to another slice of Sophie's cherry cake.

'OK. Then it's a deal?' asked Kelly.

'We will do our best to make it one,' promised Guiseppe.

Altogether too smooth, thought Dieter. A man who liked women, and knew what to say to please them. Still, a good man, and someone who was essential to the scheme.

The small producers knew him, trusted him. Kelly would need that trust before the local vineyards threw their weight behind her project.

But she was young. Could so easily become dependent. Too dependent.

'We shall give it our best shot,' he said. 'The three of us.'

Kelly smiled gratefully. Then her eyes dropped.

★ ★ ★

'I thought I'd find you out here,' said Sophie.

David looked up from the stripped-off front wheel and the dismantled brake shoe. 'I've found out why your brakes were grabbing,' he said.

Sophie sighed in exasperation. 'That could have waited. Why did you sneak off to the workshed, when Kelly was discussing her whole future?'

'This job needed doing,' he mumbled.

There was more to it than that. Hannah had unerringly found the issues causing him discomfort: the whole principle of staying on here, at the vineyard, and putting the rest of his life on hold. Doing the wrong thing, maybe, for the right reasons. Getting drawn ever deeper into the routine running of the

183

vineyard. Even asking Sergio when he should start pruning in the coming year when he should be at the other side of the world, by then, researching slave families' memories along the River Ohio. Once a good idea, now, he hadn't an ounce of interest in it.

'Kelly needed help,' scolded Sophie. 'You left her to convince everybody on her own. Sell the idea to Guiseppe and the growers' co-operative. Test Sergio's reaction, as a small producer.'

David sat back on his heels. 'What did they say?'

'They're helping her. Guiseppe and Paulo will take her round the small producers in the Langhe. Dieter's going . . . well, in case . . . '

'In case of what?'

'Guiseppe has quite a reputation. I think Dieter sees himself as a knight in shining armour, riding out to escort her safely through.'

David grinned. 'I told you he would resurface in his own time.'

'But Kelly needed *your* moral support. *Your* advice.'

'Not so,' said David. 'We talked it through when I brought her here from the airport. The idea is sound. Britain is becoming a nation of wine drinkers, and Italy is a popular base to stay or come on holiday. There will be lots of interest in decent Italian wines. Kelly has the business education. She's on fire about the whole thing. It fits like a glove the dream she has of spending her life working in a different culture. Quality before profit. Self-sustaining production, before rip-out and exploitation. Small guys, not giant corporations. I told her to go for it.'

And he'd argued her into accepting an interest-free loan from him, as part of the working capital she would need, to set up her own small wine-marketing business. But that was between the two of them.

'You should have said.'

'I just did.'

'Sorry,' Sophie said. 'It's the red hair. I go off at half-cock.'

'So will your brakes, unless we replace them.'

Sophie stared at the rusting components. So long as the car started, when she turned the key, went where she aimed, and stopped roughly where she wanted, what was the problem? There were more important things on her mind. Her cheeks coloured. 'I wanted to thank you,' she said.

'What for?'

'For everything. The work you did on the harvest. The work you've done on the wine. The way you bring Sara out of herself and laughing, so that I scarcely recognize my own daughter. The way even Hannah rates you — '

'What?' he exclaimed, astonished.

'You've made a big impression on her. That one's as hard as nails,' she said, admiration all over her face. My guess is that she tried to bounce you into doing something, but you dug in your heels and refused.'

'She's very forthright,' he mumbled.

'She's a spoiled, scheming, unprincipled, little madam.'

There was no answer to that. David wiped his hands on a rag. 'What are you holding behind your back?' he asked. 'As if I'm not meant to see it.'

He wasn't. Not now, when she had lost her courage.

Shamefacedly, she held it out.

'It's mistletoe,' he said.

'*Vischio*, they call it, over here. I was looking for a place to hang it.'

'In the workshed?'

'Everywhere else is decorated.'

He took it from her fingers, held it up towards the ceiling beam. 'Will I hang it there . . . or here . . . ?' He moved it directly over their heads.

Sophie stood on tiptoe. Kissed him. 'That's

just for tonight. And only to say thanks,' she said breathlessly.

'I understand.'

'There's no promises ... I don't even know what I'm trying to say ... '

He leaned down quietly and kissed her again.

'I'm not ready for another relationship, David. I'm too scared.'

His arms slid slowly around her. She opened her mouth to say something else, and he kissed her. Not fiercely, not possessively. Just with care, with sensitivity, as if he was handling a frightened animal who might bolt away.

Sophie kissed him back. Then forgot what she was trying to say.

Outside, Bert and Mary stood guiltily in the doorway. Then, retreated, quiet as church mice, on tiptoes, back into the dark outside the kitchen door. They had been out for a walk on the valley road in the soft glow of starlight, then been drawn by the voices from the workshed, wondering if David was there.

'I should have thought of that myself,' said Mary.

'Thought of what?' asked Bert.

'This bit of mistletoe. I saved it from the decorations.'

'What mistletoe? Where?' Bert peered in the dark.

'Up here.' She held the imaginary sprig above them.

He peered up. 'Can't see any mistletoe,' he complained.

'It's too dark. But it's there. Trust me.'

'Oh well then.' He looked at her and grinned. 'Fancy a quick snog?'

'You're such a romantic, Bert,' she sighed.

★　★　★

The tannoy system blared across Turin airport. Announcements in three different languages. He could speak all three. He was a tall man, dressed immaculately in a grey suit, woollen coat folded neatly over his arm. He walked like an athlete, fast, purposeful. The crowd, unthinking, parted to let him through. He never saw them.

He glanced at the car keys and parking number in his hand. It would be at the nearest side of the enclosure. The most expensive hired cars were always parked where the patrons could find them and exit easily. And this was a Merc.

He stopped suddenly. Flowers.

Options: buy at the airport, or gamble that he would find a flower shop still open in Alba late on Christmas Eve. Instant weighing of probabilities, and decision: he spun on his heel and strode back to the airport shops. Of course, he would be ripped off there, but he was buying for ostentation anyway — although perhaps it would be crass to leave the price tag on the flowers.

He bought the best, casually paying with plastic. Found the grey Merc in its bay and tossed the wrapped-up flowers onto the back seat. His travel case went into a boot so huge it seemed lost within it.

When you're broke, go out and hire a Rolls Royce, his father once told him.

He slid into the driving seat, reached into his pocket and brought out a case of expensive cheroots. Lit one with a gold lighter. The scented smoke swirled round his head. He couldn't do the Rolls Royce, but the rest was still impressive.

The thin lips twitched. Not a smile. Or if it was, it didn't reach his eyes.

He turned the key in the ignition, checked for traffic, then floored the accelerator and headed south.

8

Lighting a fire in the best room was a waste of time, Sophie thought ruefully. In spite of the glittering decorations, the Christmas tree with its tinsel and the brightly coloured parcels underneath, the extra comfort of the old armchairs and settees . . . one by one people had drifted through to join her in the kitchen, pulling up chairs from the old oak table, to sit in a quiet circle round the fire.

The kitchen, with its dark intricately-carved Italian furniture, and its ancient clock ticking slowly over everyone, was the heart of the house. The place where, for generations, people came instinctively to chat or simply relax, like now.

'You can't beat a real log fire,' Bert said contentedly, reaching with the poker to nudge two half-burned logs together, triggering a fresh shower of sparks and flames up the chimney. 'Beats coal. Beats central heating.'

Mary twisted in the chair, toasting her legs from a different angle. David and Sophie were sitting just a little too far apart, she thought wryly. But she was glad for her son. It was long overdue that he should move on from his wife's death, and she liked everything she had seen of Sophie — you learn quickest about people when their backs are against the wall. Sophie was OK.

She glanced at Kelly, talking quietly over the kitchen table to Dieter: her granddaughter was smitten, she thought. And she could do a whole lot worse than the gentle giant. Since the three of them had rescued one another from the flooded caravan park, there had been a quiet and steady bond of affection between herself and Bert and Dieter. She was comfortable with his long silences; guessed that there was a well-educated mind behind the drifter's exterior.

As for Sophie's daughters, they were chalk and cheese. Sara, quiet and withdrawn but shy, not stupid. Hannah, a little minx, sharp enough to cut herself. At first she suspected a malicious streak in the girl then, on better acquaintance, had been the good side too, the quick humour, the lightning-fast understanding. Not so much malicious as unprincipled, she decided. Too used to getting her own way, and too ready to make sure she did — by whatever means.

Sophie glanced up at the clock. It was well after 11.00 p.m., and she wasn't sure whether people would head off to bed or stay to listen to the radio Christmas service — if she could

191

get it on BBC World Service. From outside came the sound of a big car climbing quietly but fast up the valley road. Who on earth was getting city visitors at this time of night? She frowned — then the frown deepened when she heard the car slow, and come smoothly through her gates into the courtyard.

'Who are you expecting?' Mary asked, surprised.

Hannah smiled secretively, her eyes on the flickering flames.

She knew, Mary thought.

'Nobody,' replied Sophie, puzzled.

'Come in, Mr Nobody,' Hannah said.

'I'll get it,' David offered.

'No. My house.' Sophie headed for the kitchen door. Just as she reached it, there was a firm knock. She opened the door. Then her free hand flew up to her mouth. 'Brian!' she exclaimed.

'Merry Christmas. Can I come in?'

Without waiting for a reply, he brushed past. A tall, athletic man in an impeccable business suit, carrying a huge bunch of exotic flowers. His light-blue eyes swept round the kitchen, pausing briefly on David, then moving on.

'Hello, poppet,' he smiled at Hannah. 'Father Christmas is here. Sorry about the missing reindeer, but my sack of presents is out in the Merc.'

He turned, offering the flowers to Sophie. 'A peace offering, Soph. Season of goodwill and all that. Peace on earth to all men. If you're short of rooms, I can crash down in the kitchen, or through in the lounge. I decided that I just wasn't up to spending Christmas on my own. Away from my family . . . '

'Merry Christmas, Daddy,' Hannah said, running over to hug him.

'You won't let them throw me out, poppet? Will you?'

Hannah pouted. 'Not until you've brought in that sack of presents.'

'Good thinking. Any chance of a coffee, or something stronger, Soph? And just who is everybody? Introduce me. I'm Brian, the prodigal husband, newly returned. I hope you haven't eaten the fatted calf already.'

The words were light but Mary sensed the flat challenge behind them. Knew also that Sophie was caught totally off-balance. Small wonder, if the last person on earth she wanted to see had turned up to spoil her feast.

'I'll make the coffee, Sophie,' she offered, rising.

'Good-oh. A fresh pot, so that everyone can

join in.' Brian towered over them, smiling. 'Now, just who are you?' he asked Bert.

Sophie placed the flowers on the kitchen table, and found her voice. 'Brian,' she said, 'I told you not to come. This is totally unacceptable.'

Brian made his eyes big, in mock amazement. 'No room at the inn?'

'I simply do not want you here,' Sophie said firmly. 'And you're not going to bulldoze me into staying. Tonight, or any other night. On any pretext.'

Brian smiled. 'There must be an escape clause in the small print? Room for negotiation? After all, the girls are my children every bit as much as yours.'

Hannah smiled tightly: Mary sensed she was enjoying the battle.

'Please go,' said Sophie. 'This is ruining our Christmas.'

'If you send me out heartlessly, then you're ruining mine.'

He was enjoying this too, Mary realized. Relishing Sophie's shock and the embarrassment of her guests at being present during a family row. She filled the kettle and banged it down firmly on the burners. Why did the great put-down lines always come too late to be of any use, she thought bitterly? David was hamstrung because Brian had played the family card, blocking any external help. And Sophie looked as if she had been out-argued and out-manoeuvred so often that she didn't know how to mount any sort of counter-attack.

'Do you want us to leave you for a bit, to talk things through?' she asked Sophie. 'Or would you rather have us here?'

'Here is good,' said Brian. 'Make yourselves at home. Oh, sorry, you already have.' He smiled brightly.

'That's it!' said Sophie. 'Brian, if you have anything to say, we'll go through to the front room and talk about it sensibly. I will not have you mocking my guests — they have more right to be in this house than you have.'

'You invited me in.'

'You invited yourself in. And now, I am asking you to leave because you have come here deliberately to make a scene. Cause trouble.'

'Attagirl,' said Mary. Then sniffed, as Brian's eyes locked on her. She refused to flinch. 'You heard the lady,' she added calmly. 'Come in and behave — otherwise, there's plenty of us here to show you out.'

Brian shrugged. 'Front room it is,' he said. 'In the meantime, a happy Christmas to one and all. Bring the coffee through when it's ready.' He walked firmly to the hallway door.

'Coming, Soph?' he asked. 'There's something we need to discuss.'

★ ★ ★

David moved uneasily in his chair. The drone of the man's voice from the best room had become a dialogue. Then a heated dialogue, both voices rising. Sophie's angrily; the man speaking firmly across her.

This was Sophie's house. The man was Sophie's ex-husband, with some sort of legal claim to the girls. All David's instincts were to go through. Take her side, with enough primal male dislike to set his hackles rising, whatever the rights and wrongs of the case. But he was an outsider to the family and its disputes.

With all his heart, he wished he knew what to do.

The others sat in tense embarrassed silence. Only Hannah seemed at ease, humming quietly as she watched the fire.

'You knew he was coming,' Sara accused.

Hannah shrugged. 'I thought it was on the cards.'

'You know how they fight!'

''Through conflict comes resolution',' Hannah quoted.

'What's he talking about through there? Is it us?'

'More likely about them. The future of the vineyard. The options open.'

David's shoulders hunched; he was ready to explode, but this was not his fight.

Yes, it was. From the *vischio* moment onwards, if not before.

He rose slowly from his chair to find Sergio already standing and listening to the voices shouting through in the front room. Their eyes met.

'Come, David,' Sergio said. 'We have valley work to do.'

David nodded.

'Me too,' said Dieter, quietly. 'I go to keep the peace.'

'His choice,' growled David.

'Wrong. The man has engineered this. There must be no violence. Do not give him what he has clearly come to provoke. We shall stay peaceable, whatever he says. And simply ask him to leave, if this is what Sophie wants.'

David grunted. His whole being focused on getting into that room and standing by Sophie's side. Nature could take its course from there. He reached the door to the front room, hesitated, then opened it and walked in without knocking.

'What's the problem, Sophie?' he asked.

The man towered over her, frozen in the act of waving a finger in her face, making some point. His manner was cold, where it should have been hot. The heat all came from on Sophie's side. Sitting, her face flushed and her eyes flashing, anything but cowed. That red-haired temper had kicked in, well and truly.

'I don't recall inviting you in,' Brian said.

'We invited ourselves,' David said thickly. 'Back off. Away from Sophie.'

The man's eyes gleamed, clearly tempted. But he stepped away, and sat down in his chair again. 'Notice. No violence,' he said. 'This is a personal matter, and nothing to do with anyone else other than Sophie and myself. Please leave.'

David walked over to Sophie. 'Do you want him here?' he asked.

'I want him to go,' said Sophie. 'I'm not interested in his proposition. I don't want any further discussion. I want him to go away, and leave us in peace.'

'You heard,' growled David.

Brian leaned back comfortably. 'I hear a physical threat. What are you going to do next?' he asked. 'Throw me out? A gang of three, against a single person — someone who has every right to be in his own home.'

'My home!' cried Sophie.

Dieter pushed past David, the big arm moving him aside easily as if he was a child.

'The person who owns the house has asked you reasonably to leave,' he said quietly. 'We are her guests and advise you to do as she says. Under both Italian and British law, we are entitled to use reasonable force should you refuse.'

'So you claim.'

'Trust me. I am a lawyer, trained in both British and European law.'

'Then throw me out,' taunted Brian.

Sergio spoke for the first time, his words beyond David's limited grasp of the local French/Italian *patois*. 'Listen,' he rumbled. 'You will remember enough of our language to understand me. I neither know, nor care what the others said. This is the valley's message to you. There is a simple choice: you can leave on your feet, with the three of us escorting you, or be dragged through the kitchen in front of your children. One phone call will bring out the valley men to take you back to your hotel, or the airport. In this valley, we do not like a single part of you, and would welcome the chance to put our hands on you. *Capisce?*'

Brian flushed. He had enough confidence in himself to take on two or three of them in a primitive brawl. A little blood, a few bruises would improve his case with the local police. But the valley men were different. The only law they recognized was their own. Their punishment was brutal. And Sergio's warning was no idle threat: there was no love lost between him and them.

Weighing of options: instant decision. He could get what he wanted without shedding blood. Move directly into the second phase of his plan. So be it.

'Very well,' he said. 'You have been careful to make the threat where there are no witnesses. However, there is no need for violence. I am leaving voluntarily and without an escort. No ... *reasonable force* .... I shall go, now.'

They made a strange procession through to the kitchen.

Brian paused. 'Change of plan, poppet,' he called to Hannah. 'Coming down to the town with me? Then back on a plane, to London?'

Same rapid weighing of options, the presents piled high beneath the Christmas tree. Same instant decision. 'I think I'll stay, Daddy,' she said. 'Until the holiday is over, anyway. I'll drop in and see you on our way back to school.'

'Good-oh.' Brian paused, at the kitchen table. Then he picked up the flowers.

With an ironic flourish, he offered them to Mary. 'Seems such a shame to waste them,' he said easily. 'Have a lovely Christmas . . . at my expense . . . '

Turning on his heel, he left. They heard the muted roar of the big engine starting up. Then the growl as its revs rose, and the Mercedes pulled away. The engine noise faded, as it ghosted down the valley road.

'I could kill for a cup of tea,' said Bert.

'I'll boil the kettle again,' Mary said.

She rose, and the expensive flowers slid from her lap to the floor. Carefully, as she headed over to the kettle, she accidentally stood on them.

'Oops!' she said. 'That was clumsy, wasn't it?'

★　★　★

Kelly's head was spinning. All week, Guiseppe had driven her around the Langhe and its wine valleys. Along narrow, single-track roads which climbed up to small and ancient villages perched high on the ridges of the hills. Edging through tight muddy streets that wriggled around houses which were hundreds of years old; then dipping down into the next wine valley, and the next.

The different vineyards had gradually blended, one into the other. The various wine producers into the same dark, weather-beaten face, frowning in concentration, asking the same sharp questions. The same weighing-up look, the same glance to Guiseppe for reassurance, then the hand offered silently in a firm handshake to seal the deal.

She was starting to worry that she was gathering too much wine to sell. She said as much to Guiseppe, who shook his head.

'The level of sales don't count, first time round,' he said. 'What does is that you have visited every producer in every winery in the Langhe. Asked everyone to join. The co-operative spirit is strong among these people. But before they join together, they must see your face, listen to your offer, and decide to trust you.'

He went back into the winery, to speak to the producer.

Dieter watched Kelly bite her lip. 'Courage! You are launching a new form of co-operation,' he said quietly. 'Not just small growers bringing grapes to be made into collective wine, but small independent wineries, selling their wines collectively. These are businessmen, and won't be expecting miracles — it takes time to build a new market. They are thinking long term. And it's not a huge risk for them to take. If you don't sell their wine, it is already lying as surplus in their cellars.'

Kelly ran a troubled hand through her hair.

'I'm scared I'll only let them down,' she said. 'After raising everybody's expectations.'

'You won't let anybody down.'

She looked up at him. 'How can you possibly know that?'

The reserved face relaxed into a smile. 'Because I know you, your father, your grandfather and your grandmother. There is a family gene that won't let you be defeated. You will always find a way to be successful.'

Kelly shivered. The cold air of the valleys from a wind that travelled over some of the highest snow-covered Alpine peaks in Europe, ate into the bones.

Dieter slipped off his thick woollen scarf. 'Here,' he offered. 'I warned you that it would be cold today — despite the sun.'

'I should have listened.' Kelly wrapped the scarf round her neck. Dieter reached across, and quietly turned up her jacket collar. 'That's better,' she said. 'I feel warmer now.' And she did — for the small gesture, even more than his scarf.

'Why don't we get into the car, and wait for Guiseppe there?' he asked.

'It wouldn't be polite. He has worked so hard to make this project happen.'

Dieter grunted. He had his own views on Guiseppe's new work ethic.

'Here he comes,' said Kelly.

Guiseppe emerged from the cellars, shook the owner's hand, then trotted over. 'Another one on board,' he said cheerfully. 'He was only asking how we would collect and hold his wine at *La Co-operativa*.' He grinned at Kelly. 'If this scheme of yours takes off, I can see us having to invest in new warehousing space.'

'I'm sorry to be causing so much trouble. In your holidays too.'

'Paulo would only be dragging me out to some new local *ristorante*. This is more fun.' Guiseppe glanced at his car keys, then over at Dieter. 'Want to drive?' he asked. 'It will let you stretch these long legs of yours. I'm smaller. Plenty room for me in the back with Kelly.'

The two men's eyes locked. Dieter shook his head.

'You know the way,' he said. 'It will be quicker with you driving. I shall sit in the back, with Kelly . . . '

★ ★ ★

'Well, you should be a whole lot safer, now.' David sat on his heels, reaching for a rag to wipe the worst of the muck off his hands, the new brake assemblies fitted.

'Thanks,' said Sophie. She looked up at the

204

vischio, still fixed to its roof beam. 'And thanks for not pushing . . . after us kissing out here.'

'That was a one-off event,' David smiled. 'You warned me.'

'Even so, I feel pretty bad about it,' Sophie said quietly. 'I'm in such a mess, emotionally. Too vulnerable. Not ready to get involved again. Not yet.'

'I understand,' he said.

'I don't want to lurch into something that leaves one or both of us hurt. And I don't want to destroy our friendship. That means so much to me.'

'And me.' He headed for the Swarfega and began to work the oil and grease off his hands. 'It probably helped, to clarify things. I suppose the attraction has always been there. The *vischio* only brought it out into the open, leaving no need to tiptoe round it. We know how the other feels, but value what we already have.'

'Exactly.'

Sophie watched him wash his hands under the workshed tap.

'It's not just the car you've made safer,' she said. 'You've managed to turn things round — both the vineyard and me. Everything was spiralling out of control, before you came. But you broke the crisis down into steps that anybody could understand. Made decisions easy to take. Turned failure into success. Now we're facing spring and summer just like any other vineyard in the valley. It's all under control again. I couldn't have done that on my own.'

'You were doing just fine. Your only problem was that you were short on numbers for the harvesting.'

'Not true. I was short on planning, short on answers, short on self-belief.'

'Water below the bridge,' he said easily. 'Who was the guy in the Bible who always pitched his tent each night to leave it facing the sunrise? So that the first thing he saw each day was the new dawn with its new challenges? Meaning that any past actions are history, and each day brings a chance to do better.'

'Was it Abraham? Jacob?' Sophie asked.

'Don't know. All I remember is the message: live life one day at a time and don't be afraid to try again and again.'

As always, he was good for her, with his upbeat view on life. His stories always made things so easy to grasp. 'Don't dwell on mistakes,' she said. 'Today and tomorrow give us fresh opportunities.'

'Absolutely.'

'Did Old Testament patriarchs make mistakes like us?'

'They were human like us, so why not?'

Sophie frowned. 'We're supposed to learn from our mistakes,' she said. 'But that's just it: I don't know where I went wrong, David. I don't know what I did to make my marriage go sour. That scares me. Because if I don't know what was wrong, I could make the same mistake again. And lose you. Destroy us. Bring down everything that we're rebuilding together.'

There was raw hurt in her voice.

'Hey! We all make mistakes,' David said unsteadily. 'When I'm working on research, or writing a new course of lectures, I go obsessive. Forget everything in the world outside — including people who have every right to depend on me. Forget things, because my mind is so full of the issues and ideas I'm working with.'

His back to her, he leaned on his fists over the workbench. 'That caused rows, right through my marriage. One night, I came home really late and had forgotten that we'd planned to go out together. It was one mistake too many. My wife went ballistic, and stormed out to drive around in the car. That was her usual way of cooling down. Only this time, she hit a tree. She never came back. And I never had the chance to say to her that I was truly, deeply sorry.'

Silence settled over them both, then he turned to face her.

'You worry, because you don't know which mistake you made. Well, I know my mistake, but I also know that I could make the same mistake again. Hurt someone else whom I love with all my heart. It's not just you who's scared: we're both scared, Sophie. Both of us are badly scarred . . .'

'What can we do about it?' Sophie asked.

'Pitch our tents to face the dawn,' David said simply.

'You mean take things, one step at a time? Try to forget the past? Don't push, just give the future, the new dawns, a fair chance to work their magic?'

'Exactly,' David said. 'Take each day on trust. A new start.'

'Can we really do that?' Sophie asked. 'Is it possible?'

David shrugged. 'We won't know until we try.'

'Then it's a deal,' Sophie said quietly. 'Let's take it a day at a time. Not worry, not push. Leave the past and the future to take care of themselves.'

* * *

Sergio glanced up the vineyard slope as some flakes of clay slithered down, and grinned: 'Here's your little shadow,' he said.

David turned to see Sara slithering down the steep slope. 'Watch your feet,' he called. 'The frost has left the clay like ball bearings.'

'What are you both doing?' she panted.

'Sergio's going to show me how to prune the vines for spring.'

'Can I watch, please?'

'Didn't you see your mother do it last year?'

'She pruned in February. We were at school by then . . . ' Her feet slipped as the clay rolled and she grabbed at Sergio for balance.

He calmly fielded her. 'Take care,' he said. 'What would your mother say, if we brought you home with a broken leg?'

'If I broke my leg then I wouldn't have to go back to school,' she said. Her Italian *patois* was much more fluent than David's had yet become. He struggled to follow the liquid flow of their conversation.

Sergio released his grip. 'We could always send you to school in Alba.'

'Yes, please.'

Sergio fished in his grubby jacket for his

secateurs. 'You could do worse,' he commented. 'Here, our school is linked to college.
And you could choose to finish off your
education with the viniculture course.'

'They could teach me to become a
grower?'

He shook his head. 'No. *I* could teach you
to become a grower; any man in the valley
could teach you to become a grower. They
would teach you to become an *expert* grower,
to know as much about the biochemistry of
vines as Paulo does.'

'Gosh!' Sara said. 'Is that true, David?'

'If Sergio says so,' he answered gravely,
having understood less than half their
conversation and guessed the rest. 'You can
start your studies now, like me, with Sergio as
your tutor.'

'Do I get paid for taking on this extra
student?' Sergio demanded.

'You asked me to look at your wheel
bearings,' David smiled. 'Your ancestors
called this a *quid pro quo*. Something in
return for something else.'

'Then I will teach you both, just as my
grandfather taught me.' Sergio squatted down
in front of a ragged and blackened winter
vine. 'In the shadow of the Old Ones,' he
rumbled. 'Let them guide this work.'

He glanced up. 'To prune a vine, you must

210

separate it into a past, a present, and a future.' His blunt fingers traced the shoots from the previous year's growth and selected the thickest and most vigorous one. 'First, find the shoot which shows the greatest strength and courage. This is the vine which will put food on your table by growing grapes for you this summer. It is your *present*. But we must control its power. Cut it back to nine buds . . . so. At an angle, to help it shed the rain. Then bend it gently and tie it to your trellis wire . . . like this . . . '

He eased the shoot into a gentle arc along the wire, and tied it there. 'Next, pick the shoot that will be your *future*, the vine that will carry your hopes and prayers into the years to come. Let the Old Ones guide your hand. This shoot. Prune it back to three buds . . . so . . . Then tie it down.'

'And the rest?' David asked.

'The rest are the *past*. They have no more use. Cut them clear of the main stem, and haul them out . . . ' Sergio clipped busily, then stood up to haul away the discarded tendrils of vine. Gathering them up, he stepped back.

All that was left was a sparse, pruned vine with two small shoots.

Sergio squatted onto his heels again. 'The pruning is now finished. We have a *present*

211

shoot, that one, for David and Sophie. And we have a *future* shoot, this one, which will carry the vineyard's hopes and dreams. This is Sara's vine.'

David heard the girl gulp beside him. 'My vine? Truly? Will both of you be there to help me in that future?' she asked unsteadily.

'*Sempre,*' Sergio rumbled. 'The whole valley will help. I promise.'

'And you, David?' she asked. In English.

'Always,' he replied quietly. 'If you ever need me.'

Sergio rose stiffly. 'Lesson over. The words are my grandfather's, and have been passed down from generation to generation, since time began.' He smiled down at Sara. 'These words are the poetry, little one. Reality is different. After days and weeks of pruning, your back will be ready to snap like a twig. And your hands will blister and bleed — far worse than at any harvest. You will curse the day you were born, to tend the vines.'

'Then why do it?' Sara asked.

'Because you were born to do it,' he answered deeply. 'As that man is, at your side. Although he doesn't know this yet.'

'What did he say?' asked David, his translation lagging so far behind the flow that he had finally given up.

'I will tell you,' Sara said. 'One day, when the time is right.'

★ ★ ★

'It's the postman,' said Bert, looking out of the kitchen window. 'I thought I recognized the van. I'll get it.' He headed out for the mail.

'Where's David?' Mary asked.

'On the slopes with Sergio.'

'And Sara?'

Hannah glanced from her book. 'Find David and you will find them both.'

Bert returned to the kitchen. 'Here's one with a London stamp. This posh one.' He held up an expensive white envelope with a company logo. 'I bet that's where half their profits go,' he said. 'No Tesco envelopes for these boys.'

'Let me see,' said Sophie. She took the mail, glanced through the others, then dropped them onto the kitchen table. 'Who on earth is writing to me from London?' she asked, puzzled. That belonged to another life.

Moving into the greater light of the window, she eased open the flap. They watched her slide out a single sheet of thick paper. 'It's from a firm of London lawyers,' she muttered. Then began to read.

Mary saw her sway, and Bert reached out to steady her.

'They can't!' Sophie whispered. 'They absolutely can't.'

She stared at them ashen-faced. 'How could he do this to me?'

'Who? Do what?' asked Bert.

Tears welled in Sophie's eyes. 'It's Brian,' she said. 'When he was over on Christmas Eve, he was trying to persuade me to close down the vineyard. He told me that it was rundown, ancient. That no one would ever make a living from it. He wanted to rip out the vines, and use the land for something else.'

'What?' asked Mary.

'Property development. Some mad scheme he has to build a load of holiday and retirement homes. For monied Brits. With a leisure centre and a swimming pool thrown in. He wanted to get the work done now, so that we could sell fast, on the upturn. Once the economic recovery brings real growth again.'

'He can't do that,' protested Mary. 'It's your vineyard. Your house.'

Sophie held out the letter. As Mary took it uncertainly from her shaking fingers, Sophie said, 'His lawyers claim the title deeds were never transferred to my name. So Brian is now demanding his share of half the value of the villa and the vineyard, or the land for property development purposes.'

They stared at each other. Then Bert turned to the kitchen door.

'I'll get David,' he said.

9

This was another grim council of war, around the old kitchen table. As the fire sparked and crackled in the background, Sophie's strange extended family were trying to come up with a strategy to help her.

'I don't understand,' said David, pushing the lawyer's letter back across the table. 'If the divorce settlement has gone through, and he's signed the paperwork . . . then that's a binding contract. Brian can't just come back and claim half of what he has already settled on you.'

'That's my reading of it too,' said Kelly.

Dieter said nothing. He reached quietly across the table, took the letter and began to read it again, frowning.

'So Brian's just chancing his arm?' asked Mary. 'He's bound by the legal papers that he signed?'

'There are no legal papers,' Sophie said, her face colouring. 'The divorce has still to be finalized. We're separated, waiting out the time, before his lawyers can apply for the full decree.'

'That changes the whole position!' David exclaimed.

'I know,' Sophie said wretchedly. 'But he promised . . .'

Dieter folded the letter and laid it on the table. 'This promise your husband made,' he said. 'Was it in words . . . or in a written document?'

'We agreed, verbally, and he confirmed it in a letter.'

'You have this letter?'

'Somewhere . . . Shall I go for it?'

'Later.' This was a different Dieter: gone was the silent giant and in his place sat a calm professional lawyer.

'Would that letter carry the full force of a legal contract?' David asked him.

'It's in his own handwriting — and signed,' said Sophie. She ran her hands agitatedly through her hair. 'It anchored down the deal we'd made. I was to get the vineyard, because he had no interest in that. He was to take the other half — most of the savings we'd left, the stocks and shares he had invested the rest of his golden handshake into. And he was to look after the girls' education as well. It's all in the letter.'

'How much were these investments worth?' Kelly asked.

'I've no idea. Brian handled the money side

of things. I dealt with the vineyard and the cellars.'

'Not even roughly? If we can show that he has already taken half of the wealth the two of you had accumulated . . . ' Kelly looked desperately at Dieter. 'Isn't that how it works?' she asked.

Dieter gently scratched his nose. 'Yes, provided that it was part of the legal settlement,' he finally replied. 'Agreed in the legal paperwork. But this was an informal agreement between the parties, well in advance of the final decree.'

'An agreement is surely still an agreement,' David argued.

'Yes and no.' Dieter touched the letter again. 'This is something he has already settled with his legal team — or they would not have worded the letter as they have, asking for half the value of the vineyard, its cellars, and the villa.'

'What do you mean?' David asked.

'He's got caught out with all his fancy deals on the stock market,' Sophie interrupted angrily. 'I think his investments have gone down, when everything tumbled after the credit crunch. I think he's broke, and trying to raid my money.'

Dieter waited patiently.

'What do you think?' she demanded.

'You're our expert.'

'I think his legal team will argue that the original letter should not stand,' Dieter said. 'They will say that it was written when their client was distraught — his mind confused by grief and guilt at the breakdown of his marriage. They will argue that, in the spirit of natural justice, his impetuous letter should be set aside, and the two parties should make a standard settlement based on an equal share of their *current* financial and other assets. That's the normal pattern — equal shares.'

'He *can't* have done this!' Sara hissed at Hannah. 'Not even Daddy!'

'It looks as if he has,' Hannah replied, and settled back.

'But they can't set aside his promise!' Sophie said desperately.

'Not if he's already lost his own share,' Mary backed her up.

'As yet, there is no divorce,' Dieter said. 'Both parties are merely separated and technically still married. It doesn't matter what he took, and what he did with it in the past. Only what he and Sophie own *now*, because these are the assets available for sharing. Courts aren't interested in claims and counter-claims from before the hearing. They hold these at arm's length, to reach an objective solution.'

'How can you be so sure his lawyers will take that line?' David asked.

'Because it is exactly what I would be arguing for any client of mine.'

'Even if it distorts the settlement in favour of your client?'

'A lawyer is employed to act in his client's best interests. To present the facts in the best possible light. To use whatever legal principles are appropriate.'

'That's immoral!' Mary exclaimed.

Dieter shrugged. 'If you employed me to protect you, would you want me to stand up in court and admit that your opponent held the moral high ground?'

In the silent kitchen, the old clock ticked on slowly.

'Then I'm as good as done for,' Sophie said quietly.

Dieter held up his hands. 'Any legal system is adversarial. I was only stating the argument that Brian's legal team are likely to use. You will have your own legal team. They will research everything, and come up with their own counter-arguments, their own set of legal principles, to support your case.'

'Then I can still fight this' — Sophie angrily knocked the letter off the table — 'this thing? This unprincipled grab at my house, my vineyard?'

Dieter calmly picked the letter off the floor. 'Oh yes, you can fight,' he said.

'How? What can I do? Tell me, please?'

Dieter frowned. 'If you were my client, I would try to find proof that Brian has frittered away the share of wealth he took in your informal settlement. I would seek to damage his character. Then I would turn the argument for natural justice on its head, and argue what right has a man like that to come back and steal what he has already freely given?'

Sophie's nostrils flared. 'All I ask is a fair fight,' she said.

Dieter smiled wryly. 'Then the last place you'll find it is in a court of law.'

The clock ticked on.

'Can you defend me, Dieter?'

Dieter placed a finger on the still-crisp notepaper, and slowly spun the letter round on the table. Then looked up. 'It is a past that I have been running away from,' he said quietly. 'But yes, for a friend, I will go back.'

He sighed. 'I shall contact my father's legal business up in Munich. They should act officially in your defence. My father has legal associates in London. I used to shuttle back and forwards — that was my job, handling British law cases for our European clients. I will return to London and work with them to probe what Brian has been doing with his money. There is something rotten there, I think.'

'What can we do in the meantime?' Sophie demanded, standing up because she could bear to sit no longer.

Dieter gently waved her down. 'We will start with facts,' he said. 'Go right back to the beginning and tell me about how much it cost you to buy the villa and its land. How much you both spent on it, to re-equip the cellars with more modern fermentation vats. How much Brian got in that golden handshake. How much you remember holding in every account in banks and building societies.'

Sophie sat down. 'How can I possibly remember all of that?' she asked.

Dieter smiled at her, from across the table.

'You will, Sophie . . . because you must,' he said simply.

★　★　★

'You heard what Dieter said,' Mary muttered. 'We'll get no justice from a court of law. Brian will have hired the fanciest lawyers in town. They'll run rings round us.'

She lapsed into silence, staring gloomily through their bedroom window. This over-looked the valley, where low winter sunshine outlined in silver the endless geometry of vine trellises. Although it was a view she loved, Mary didn't see it.

Bert waited patiently, an open book on his lap.

The sun turned her silver hair into a halo. 'So, if the courts won't help us, we'll have to make our own justice,' she mumbled.

'How?'

'Don't know.' She stared down the valley. 'It's nothing less than theft, what Brian is up to. He shouldn't get away with it. If Dieter's right, the court will split their wealth fifty-fifty, and that will wipe Sophie out. If she keeps the villa, that's worth at least as much as the vineyard land, maybe more. And Brian will get what he's looking for, all these slopes above the valley, to turn into holiday homes and a leisure club.'

Bert gently closed his book. 'He's stealing land,' he said.

'Of course he is.'

'And peasant farmers have fought and died for their land, since time began.'

Mary turned slowly, her eyes narrowing in thought.

'That's your cause,' Bert said. 'Every crusade needs a cause.'

'Bert,' she said, 'you're not just a pretty face.'

'I'm not much else.'

'You're a genius. We launch a crusade. Whip up public opinion and a sense of outrage. Publicize what he's doing. Shame him, humiliate him into backing off . . . '

'How?' Bert asked.

Mary sighed. 'I was hoping you had the answer to that.'

'Two old wrinklies aren't much of a crusade.'

Mary's face came alive again. 'We can do much better than two!' she exclaimed. 'We'll get Sergio to line up all the valley people on Sophie's side.'

'We could march,' Bert said slowly. 'Like the Jarrow Marchers. Hold up the traffic and attract the newspapers, to see what we're protesting about.'

'Not just this valley,' Mary said intensely. 'What about the other wine valleys? Land is land, and small farmers everywhere will join us. All these wine producers that Kelly is helping . . . maybe we can ask them to help us with this protest, in return. We need Guiseppe to tell us what to do. He'll know how to contact people. He'll know how to get the newspapers involved.'

She paused. 'Bert? Where are you off to?'

Bert turned at the bedroom door. 'Getting Kelly,' he said. 'If it's Guiseppe's help you're after, then Kelly's the one to bring him on board. Not us.'

★ ★ ★

'What's biting you?' asked Kelly.

Dieter looked up, startled, from his walk. Then smiled. 'Hi, Kelly.'

'Hiya.' She dropped in alongside him. 'You look as if all the worries in the world are on your shoulders.'

'Close,' said Dieter.

They climbed companionably together up the valley road, endless lines of winter-dead vines on either side of them. 'Well?' Kelly prompted.

Dieter stopped. 'I'm scared,' he said.

'You? Scared?'

The grey eyes crinkled. 'Oh yes. Me.'

'Of what?'

Dieter shrugged. 'Going back to the law,' he said. 'How much have I forgotten? Is there still an edge? Can I break through people's guard, and turn their words against them? I am a different person now. If that edge is gone, then Brian's lawyers will defeat us. Our case is weak. Sophie stands to lose almost everything — the vineyard, certainly.'

'You'll find a way to stop them.'

'How can you know that?' he asked.

225

'I asked you the same question, two days ago, and you answered; because I know you, and have faith that you will find a way to succeed. The same answer now applies to you.'

Dieter bowed his head. 'Thank you,' he said. 'But Brian and his lawyers will not give in easily. I sense the gamble of a desperate man. I think his whole future might depend on winning this. It will be a dirty fight.'

'Get your retaliation in first. Find something out about his background, about what happened to his own share of the settlement. Cut the ground from under him, leave him with no place to hide.'

Dieter's eyes lifted up to the ridges of the Langhe hills. He slowed down, then stopped. 'Once I had no place to hide,' he said. 'Often, the ground was cut from beneath our feet . . . ' His voice faltered.

Kelly hesitated, then reached out and tried to turn him round to face her.

He wouldn't move.

Gathering all her courage, she walked round, to stand and face him.

'Tell me,' she said. 'Tell me what they did to you.'

He shook his head.

'I am not moving, until you do,' she said determinedly.

'Things you would not want to know.'

'Try me.'

His eyes on the soft hills beyond her, Dieter took a long shuddering breath.

'I was defence lawyer for a German NATO soldier, out on the eastern border of Afghanistan,' he said. 'He was facing court martial. We were driving out to meet him. We were kidnapped by the Taliban, our escort and myself. Taken up into the hills. Held as hostages.'

A vague memory stirred in Kelly's mind. 'They killed a German soldier when the deadline was passed for the exchange they wanted. Then, with the other hostages still missing, simply disappeared. It scarcely made our news. There were so many other hostages situations — like in Iraq. You were caught up in that?'

Dieter nodded. 'The Taliban who ambushed us were a raiding party. Their leader was an extremist. He did the execution himself. The rest of the troop were arguing among themselves. Saying he should have waited longer . . . handed us over to higher authorities in the Taliban . . . got more publicity.'

He sighed. 'Then they offloaded me and the other two soldiers to the local *mujahidin*. They took us with them back into the mountains of the east, and held us there as prisoners, until they got new instructions. But the instructions never came. The *mujahidin* drifted south, always on the fringes of the fighting. We had no food, no medicines. They suffered as badly as we did. There was always illness, fevers. Bad water, I think. The two soldiers died and I was left with a band of peasant Afghans who hadn't a word of German or English between them.'

'Did they treat you badly?'

'They treated me well. They shared their food and water with me. When I had fever, two of them would help me walk. If they had fever, it was my job to help or even carry the sick ones. We lived up on the mountain tops, always scratching for food. Always pursued by British and American planes.'

He paused. 'That's why I know what it's like, to be in the open, to have rockets fired at you that slice and melt the ground from under your feet. We were hunted like animals. By my own side.'

Kelly waited. 'Were your captors religious extremists too?' she asked.

'No. They were simple men. They had been told by their religious leaders that the Americans and British were invaders. They were fighting for their country — like the French Resistance did, like you Britons would have done if our Hitler had invaded you. These were middle-aged men and boys. Scared by the weapons of the West, terrified of the planes and helicopters. Every month, we lost men — killed by troops who were far better armed. There was no battle plan. They were simply fighting for their country. Ready to die, if that was what it took.'

'I thought the *mujahidin* were zealots, *jihadists*?'

'Not the band who held me. Their Islam was simple, kind and basic. They treated everybody but the soldiers firing on them as a fellow man.'

'Didn't they take it out on you, when some of them were killed?'

'When someone died, they were sad. I stayed apart from them until they asked me to come back and share the cave or fire with them.'

'How long did they hold you?' Kelly asked.

'Over two years.'

'In solitary confinement?'

'No. Living with men I liked. My new brothers.'

A magpie called harshly, startling her. 'How did you escape?'

'They released me. When they went down from the hills to fight, they always left me in a cave, tied up. One night they were almost wiped out, only three were left, and one of them was badly wounded. They crept back up to the cave and cut my bonds. They spoke to me. I think they were saying that they couldn't look after me any more. They led me out, and pushed me away into the dark. I felt one last pat on the back, then they were gone.'

Dieter's head drooped. 'I waited until dawn. Came down from the hills in broad daylight . . . was arrested by a troop of British boys. They handed me over to the Germans. There was a huge celebration in Germany . . . but it meant nothing to me. I had changed. I missed my brothers and their simple honest values. I was lonely, estranged, lost in my own country.'

At last, his eyes came up and found her. She saw silent tears in them.

'I drifted,' he said. 'I no longer fit in, anywhere. Until I came here.'

Kelly's vision blurred. Impulsively, she took one of his huge hands.

'You're not lost,' she said. 'You've been found. The Old Ones searched the world for you and have brought you home.'

Dieter looked at her small hands closed over his.

'Sophie was right,' he said quietly.

'Why? What do you mean.'

'Something she said. It doesn't matter.' He

studied her, as if seeing her for the first time. Black hair, a face that sun and wind would never tan. Eyes intense and full of life. His heart turned over. The story had come tumbling out as if it had finally found the one person who would listen and understand. Feel the same.

Kelly felt the gentle scrutiny. Blushed.

'Come on,' she said. 'We both have things to do. I have wine to sell.'

Dieter smiled, a slow-burning smile which lit up his face — and her heart.

'While I go to London,' he said, 'to prepare for battle.'

'To fight for Sophie.'

'For Sophie, yes. But also, not to disappoint your trust.'

'You will never do that,' Kelly said.

★ ★ ★

'This doesn't feel right,' Bert said dismally. 'What are we doing in a place like this?'

'Wheest!' said Mary. 'The receptionist will hear you.'

'I know how you feel,' whispered Sophie. 'This place intimidates me.'

She glanced round the high-tech office: all smoked glass with matt-finished metalwork. Outside the triple-glazed windows the dense

Milan traffic flowed past silently. Like the background for a movie-shoot, everything felt unreal, false. Far from the valley culture. Too far, maybe.

'I wish Guiseppe had come,' Mary muttered. 'This guy's his friend.'

'With Kelly back selling wine in Scotland, there was no chance of Guiseppe coming here,' Bert said. 'At least he's rounding up support from the Langhe's wine valleys. The rest is up to us.'

They subsided into uneasy silence. Guiseppe had listened, weighed up the options, agreed: their only chance was to play upon emotions and take the battle out beyond the courtroom walls. Publicity and scandal. But that was not his scene, he was just a wine co-operative manager. He'd stared through the dusty windows of his office then reached for the phone to make a call. Five minutes later he'd set the phone down gently. There was a friend, a specialist in this sort of thing, a top line publicity agent. A busy man, but one who had listened, argued, then agreed to see them. And then, perhaps, to do the best he could.

So here they were, waiting on a different planet from the valley they'd left behind, dropped off at the railway station by David before he headed to Turin Airport to send a protesting Sara and strangely subdued

Hannah back to their school. While Dieter, like Kelly, had left the day before.

The new family was breaking up, heading off to battle stations.

'It's such a long shot,' Sophie said, as much to herself as the others. 'I want to fight, I *need* to do something . . . I just can't sit and wait for Dieter to phone back instructions from London or Munich. But, right now, my story sounds pathetic.'

Mary reached out, covering Sophie's hand with her own.

'We'll fight,' she said firmly. 'Long shot or not, we're going for it. If we can just get the ball rolling on the crusade . . . get enough people out behind us on a march . . . then I feel it in my bones, that's our only way of getting justice.'

Would anyone ever notice, Sophie wondered bleakly? If they did, would they even care? 'Sure,' she said. 'We've come this far. Let's give it our best shot.'

★ ★ ★

Sophie should be here, David thought desperately. She would handle this one child rebellion much better than he was doing. But the future of the vineyard was more important than being at the airport. That's what he'd told her earlier today. Now he wasn't so sure.

He pointed to the Departures board above their heads. 'Look, you must go through,' he pleaded. 'There's barely enough time for the security check before your plane is boarding. Then a couple of hours and you'll be home.'

'My home is here,' said Sara. 'And it's less than two hours away.'

'But your school term starts tomorrow,' he argued.

'I could go to school in the valley. Sergio said so.'

'Your mother wouldn't wear that. Better just go back to your school and leave us to do the fighting. In any case, there's not much can be done until Dieter contacts us from London.'

'What about the pruning?' Sara asked, on the edge of tears.

'Too early for that. But I'll make a start,' said David. 'I promise.'

'I want to come home with you. To work on the vines.'

Hannah looked on, strangely quiet. None of the flip side showing.

David turned to her. 'Tell Sara that she has to go back. Please.'

'It's her life. Her choice.'

'She has to finish school before she

chooses. We all have to do that.'

'Why should school hold a monopoly on education?' countered Hannah. She turned to Sara, and gently took an arm. 'Come on, Sis,' she said quietly. 'No point in making a scene. David's only doing what he promised Mum he'd do.'

'I want to know what happens in Milan,' Sara protested.

'We'll phone you. Tonight. As soon as your mother gets home.'

Sara clung to him. 'I don't want to go,' she sobbed. 'Don't make me . . . '

David hugged her. 'We don't have any choice,' he said. 'Any of us.'

Hannah gently tugged Sara free. 'We'll miss our plane,' she said. Then she turned to David. 'Do I get a hug too?'

Surprised, he hugged her. Felt the slight increase in pressure she gave back.

'Right. Do I check my pockets now?' he teased her.

She grinned. 'I already have. There's nothing worth stealing. *Ciao*.'

'*Ciao*, Hannah,' said David. 'We'll phone tonight,' he promised Sara.

'I'll be back,' she said.

'That's what the *Terminator* said,' quipped Hannah, hauling Sara away.

David watched the crowd engulf them.

Then turned leadenly away from Departures. Blew his nose. He was missing them already — yes, *them*. Not just his shadow, Sara, but the difficult and mercurial Hannah too.

He felt in his pocket for car keys. Then took one last look at the flow of people heading through to security, half expecting to see Sara escaped and running back to him. But there was only a constant flow of strangers, carrying skis and brightly coloured bags and laptop cases. He sighed: he'd done his job.

The battlefield was cleared and ready. For its final battle.

★ ★ ★

The silence lengthened, thickened. The media guru sprawled carelessly across his high-backed chair. But there was nothing careless in the sharp eyes or face. He'd listened to Sophie making her pitch, given her barely two minutes before switching into question and answer mode. Then sat silently, fingers drumming on the highly polished desk top.

Bert twitched: this man's help was crucial.

'Is it an idea you can sell to the public?' he blurted out.

Roberto Guttieri shrugged. 'We can sell anything,' he said, in American-accented

English. Another Italian who had done finishing school abroad. 'Having a product helps, but it's not essential. Name it, and we will find the angles to use, the buttons to press. Hire actors for the marvelling crowds and get script writers to do the testimonials . . . anything is possible in our world.'

He kicked his chair back and prowled over to the glass outer wall. Hands in pockets, he stared down at the traffic which filled the street from kerb to kerb.

'We've sold better, we've sold worse,' he sighed, turning to lean nonchalantly against space. 'No offence, Sophie, but you should have come to me twenty years ago. That was my period for lost causes. Lost most of them myself, because I didn't know what I was doing. Now I have a reputation to protect . . . '

'Big deal,' muttered Mary.

Roberto smiled. 'That's what I thought too. Call me crazy, but I'm taking your project on. Not just because you're Guiseppe's friends. It's a challenge, near-impossible to orchestrate. And it's only the impossible that gets me out of bed, these days.'

Bert sighed: it came from the soles of his shoes. 'Thanks,' he said.

Roberto waved him aside, and prowled back to the desk.

'We need to be a little bit creative,' he mused. 'Tweak your story here and there. Bring some drama to it. With respect, your crusade is boring. Nobody cares about right and wrong, these days. We have to get the public looking at the *people*, not the cause. If they love *you*, they will love your cause. So, we redefine.'

He stared at Sophie. 'OK, so we have your ex coming home to steal your land. And two whole regions of grape growers at your back, with you leading them like Joan of Arc . . . '

'Maybe thirty or forty guys,' Bert said uncomfortably.

'Who cares? We run them back behind the camera, then walk them through again. Details. I have guys who are paid to organize details. It is the concept which is important.' He looked down critically. 'Bit old for the virgin Joan,' he judged, 'but good bone structure. We get them to do you three-quarter profile, high. Cuts out the double chins.'

'I don't have double chins,' Sophie protested.

'Shadows do funny things,' Roberto said. 'High camera . . . can you wear a lower neckline?'

'No,' Sophie replied firmly, folding her arms across her chest.

'What about me?' Mary asked, hitching up her bosom.

'They don't have cinemascope,' said Bert.

Roberto grinned. 'You are the crippled mother. Rising from her deathbed to fight at her daughter's side. Good angle that. It touches me.'

'I'm not her mother and I wasn't on my deathbed . . . '

Roberto ignored her. 'While *your* daughter, Sophie, is spearheading our latest export drive. Opening up the whole of Britain to Italian wine . . . '

'*My* granddaughter,' Mary snapped. 'For Heaven's sake, get your facts right.'

'Facts?' scoffed Roberto. 'These guys out there have a story to sell — facts only get in the way.' He came back to stand, frowning, over Mary. 'My instincts tell me that *this* is our major asset. We go for public sympathy. Set you in a wheelchair, with a walking stick.'

Mary's face went dark red. 'No wheelchair,' she said angrily.

'Hey,' he said. 'That's good. The anger. Channel it . . . Props . . . '

He rushed over to a cupboard set flush against the office wall, and they heard him rummaging inside. 'Got it!' he said at last. He emerged triumphant with an old-fashioned wooden walking stick. 'Used this back in the nineties,' he said. 'It won an audience in the Vatican, but it should have been an Oscar. Here, try it for size.'

He thrust the stick at Mary, then perched on the edge of his desk to judge the effect. Mary glared at the stick in her hand. It was her greatest fear: that her mini-stroke would come back as a major one leaving her trapped in a wheelchair, or limping with a walking stick for real. This charade seemed to tempt fate and invite the worst to happen. She was simultaneously frightened and furious.

Without thinking, she reversed her grip on the stick, and raised it slowly until the handle locked beneath Roberto's chin. Then pushed his head back, slowly.

'No wheelchair,' she said tightly. 'No way, José. No wheelchair. No walking stick. I protest on my own two feet, or not at all — '

Roberto's hand groped backwards for the telephone. He found it and raised it to his face. '*Trovare un dunnato fotografo! Non posso restare in questa posa per sempre . . .*'

'Mary!' Bert exclaimed, appalled.

'What's he saying?' Mary asked Sophie uncertainly. She lowered the walking stick, but Roberto grabbed it, setting it back where it had been.

Sophie smiled. 'He's asking for a photographer and telling them to hurry, because he can't hold that pose all day . . . '

Roberto rolled an eye at Bert. 'Hey, buddy. We've got a winner here. Star quality, in the raw. Forget the wheelchair image,' he said dreamily. 'I see this different, better, now.' His hand sketched a banner headline. '*La Nonna Combattimenti* — the Fighting Grandmother!'

Mary's arm dropped. Impatiently, Roberto rammed the walking stick back into position. 'Oh, I *do* like that. *She* is our focus. *She* is the one who will lead our troops. Out at the front of our column, sitting on a white horse . . . '

'Can't manage the white horse,' Bert said apologetically. Then he glanced at Sophie. 'Would a beaten up old white Fiat Punto do?'

Sophie clapped her hands. 'I'll get David to wash it specially for the occasion,' she said.

'Then it's *Thunderbirds, go,*' Roberto said. 'Where *is* that photographer?'

10

The column of tractors trundled slowly along the motorway across the plain, police outriders escorting it front and back. Perched on the metal seat of her tractor and wrapped up against the cold, Sophie shivered.

'We'd have been better with the white horse,' she said. 'Horses have softer backs to sit on. And they must be warmer, too.'

'You can keep your horse,' said Mary. 'I'd have been happier in your car, with the heater up to max — ' She broke off to wave as a stream of traffic overtook them, horns blaring. Not so much in rage, as pledging support. 'That Roberto,' she continued, 'he's a bit of a chancer — but he certainly knows how to drum-up publicity.' More cars blared past, in the opposite direction.

'Your fans,' said Sophie, ruefully.

Mary clung more firmly to her shoulders, standing on the tail plate of the tractor. 'It doesn't matter who's getting the publicity — so long as the cause is. And at least you got a new coat of white paint on your tractor.'

'They all look the same under mud,' said Sophie.

Mary craned, to look back. 'Guiseppe's done a great job for us.'

The line of tractors stretched far behind, piloted by dark, weather-beaten faces, wrapped up against the winter cold. Everybody was taking their time, because there was no rush to reach Milan. The more days they took, the longer Roberto had to press his publicity buttons. Already the story had moved from regional to national papers, and had featured a couple of interviews for regional television. Roberto's instincts had been right: their story rocketed into prominence, because the Italian public took *La Nonna Combattimenti* to their hearts.

'Italians love their grandmothers,' he had purred.

Over the noise of Sophie's tractor engine came the heavy egg-beater sound of a helicopter flying low. It swung round in front of them, hovering barely above the power lines, faces and cameras at every window.

'Give them a wave!' hissed Mary.

'You're the one who's in the running for the Oscar,' said Sophie. But she took a hand off the caterpillar levers and waved up, smiling. The tractor veered, and Mary half-fell over her. 'What are you doing up there?' Sophie demanded.

'Trying to bow,' Mary said breathlessly. 'Then you swerved.'

The din from the helicopter's engine became a solid wall of sound, as it lifted away. The wind from its blades battered against them briefly, bringing tears to the eyes. Then it droned forward steadily. Chugging along, they watched it circle, then settle down into a field at the side of the road, about half a mile away.

'More interviews,' said Mary, sounding resigned and professional.

Sophie smiled. 'Do try to get your facts right, this time,' she cautioned.

'They get lost a bit in translation,' Mary shrugged. 'Anyway, Roberto says nobody's interested in facts.'

Brian's lawyers might be, Sophie thought wryly. 'Hold tight,' she said. 'No more bowing and waving until we draw up.'

'Right. Is my hair all blown about?'

'Authenticity,' Sophie smiled. 'You're Joan of Arc, leading her warriors. Now you know why her hair was always short . . .'

She turned, following the police escort into a farm courtyard, where dozens of reporters and photographers were already waiting: yet another glimpse of the impressive organizational skills of Roberto's outfit. He was already there, she noticed, ensuring pride of place and angle for the TV coverage.

'Hi girls,' he said easily. 'Fifteen minutes of questions, then we're off in the helicopter to the TV studio. You're booked into a chat show tonight, Mary. We need to get you there and made-up, before the cameras roll. They're providing the interpreter. I'll do that duty for you here.'

He beckoned the cameras closer. 'Shake your stick at them, Mary,' he called. 'Look fierce! Be the battling grandmother! That's what they want to see.'

'The stick,' hissed Mary. 'Where did I leave it?'

Sophie sighed, lifting it from the floor. As Mary waved it around, camera flashes became blinding. Sophie was getting used to that by now and knew that it was her job to look soulful and wronged.

Mary eased herself down from the tractor step, as Bert came over to help.

'I'm so stiff,' she whispered. 'My legs are killing me, from all that standing.'

'You're a trouper,' he said. 'The show must go on.'

'Troupers only perform nightly,' she grumbled. 'I'm doing it five times a day. And now there's a TV chat show. What will I do on that?'

'What you've been doing the last forty

years without stopping to draw breath,' he told her. 'Just keep talking.'

'Ha, ha,' Mary said darkly. 'Wait till I get you, back home.' She gathered herself, then began to limp towards the reporters.

'Mary!' he hissed after her.

'What?'

'You should be limping with the other leg.'

'Oh,' she said, and changed over. There was a roar of laughter and a cheer from the ranks of the press. In their tabloid world where facts were irrelevant, they were happy to take her for what she was. A feisty character. Someone they could rely on to provide a sharp one-liner to head their column, and make the editor smile.

Mary was quickly enveloped in a good-natured maul where she made a space for herself and Roberto with a musketeer-like flourish of her walking stick.

Sophie turned to Bert. 'How does she do it?' she demanded.

'Like a duck to water,' Bert sighed. 'She's loving every minute of it. Roberto's right: it's not our crusade they've come for . . . it's her. She has half of Italy on our side already. They'll swallow any cause she's fronting.'

'Meanwhile, what about me, after they whisk you two off to the TV studio?'

Bert grinned. 'Keep driving. Somebody has

to lead the protest convoy of wine-producers to Milan. In case anybody bothers to check.'

'Nobody ever wants to interview me — yet the crusade's about *my* vineyard,' protested Sophie. Then the sheer absurdity of the whole thing struck her.

And she began to laugh.

★   ★   ★

The valley *felt* empty, David thought. Even the birdsong was muted. He leaned against the kitchen doorframe, sipping coffee and looking out. He had been left on guard while the others were crusading, and was about to make a start on pruning the vines, keeping the promise he had given to Sara.

He took another sip of coffee. Plenty of time: the chore would take them through what was left of January and February too. Once he would have rushed at the job, working at it obsessively until it was finished. But now he had tuned into the natural rhythms of the valley. And felt at peace.

David grimaced. Too much at peace. There was a whole world out there, waiting for him to make his decisions: an American university, wondering when their expected sabbatical professor would arrive to start his research; a Scottish university querying what he was doing with the time they had given him.

He didn't want to go back there. Ever.

The stark finality of the thought shocked him. Uneasily, he returned to the kitchen, setting his half-drunk mug of coffee down at the side of Sophie's kitchen sink. Drifting created a mindset where avoiding decisions became natural. But he simply couldn't leave Sophie now. Not when she was fighting for her life — or to keep hold of her house and vineyard, which was the same thing.

The telephone rang out in the hallway, startling him.

He went through to pick it up. 'Hello?'

'Can I speak to Mrs Hargreaves, please. It's urgent.'

A very posh woman's voice, used to giving commands.

'I'm sorry,' he said. 'She is somewhere on the road to Milan.'

'And to whom am I speaking?'

'David Kinsella. Professor Kinsella. A friend, who is staying here.'

He seldom used his title, but sensed the other weighing it up. Accepting.

'Moorhurst College here. Have you the means of contacting Mrs Hargreaves in an emergency, Professor Kinsella?'

'Of course.'

A sigh. 'Then I'm afraid this is just such an emergency. Please telephone her immediately, and tell her that her girls have run away from school. Hannah phoned me from London Airport. They are catching the nine-thirty flight to Turin. Arriving there about twelve forty-five your time.'

David quickly checked his watch. 'That's OK. If I leave in half an hour, I can easily drive up and collect them. I can reach Turin more quickly than their mother.'

'I would be greatly obliged.' Frosty anger, firmly controlled.

'I'm sorry,' he said. 'It was very naughty of the girls. We have a . . . crisis, here, a dispute between their parents. My guess is that one or both of the girls wanted to come back to help solve the problem. I'll field them at this end. As soon as their mother gets back, we'll return them to your school. I can only apologize on their mother's behalf.'

'Indeed. Tell Mrs Hargreaves not to send the children back without speaking to me first. We may not allow them to return to Moorhurst. Such irresponsible behaviour is completely unacceptable. Against the school's moral code.'

'Of course,' said David. 'I appreciate that. Have you telephoned their father?'

'Mrs Hargreaves is the named emergency contact.'

'Yes. But, perhaps, their father should be told. I don't have his number.'

'Very well.' The phone went dead. He stared at it, pulled a wry face, and replaced the receiver. Then he reached for his mobile phone.

★　★　★

'Right. Whose idea was it?' David demanded, thinking, as they came through the Arrivals gate, that there was none of the gleefulness of truants about them. Instead, sober faces and eyes that refused to meet his.

'Mine,' said Sara.

'It was our idea,' amended Hannah.

'Mainly mine,' Sara insisted. 'I couldn't bear being away while everybody was fighting for our vineyard. I asked Hannah to lend me the money . . . '

'She couldn't travel on her own,' said Hannah. 'Airports refuse to let single children fly. They must be accompanied by another child, or adult. Anyway' — her face came up, eyes challenging — 'Sara's hopeless at organizing flights. Somebody had to look after her.'

'Where's your luggage?' David asked. 'Have

we to pick it up at the carousel?'

'No luggage,' said Hannah. 'Just us.'

'We had to get away without attracting attention,' Sara explained. 'Make it look as if we were only going out for a walk before classes.'

David turned to Hannah. 'Where did you get the money to pay for tickets?'

She shrugged. 'Savings. Daddy's always subbing me money — and I don't want half the stuff he buys for me, so I sell it on.'

Another wheeler-dealer, like her father, David thought wryly.

'Well, you got here safely,' he said.

'You're not mad at us, are you?' For a moment, Hannah looked uncertain, very much her age.

'Not as much as I should be,' David replied. 'Just relieved your headmistress phoned in time to let me collect you.'

'That was Hannah's idea,' said Sara. 'Phoning her from the airport. We knew she'd have to phone home, and warn you.'

'What if nobody had been in? What if we had all been away on the crusade?'

'How is it going?' Sara asked eagerly. 'Have we got any publicity?'

David put an arm round each of their shoulders and steered them to the airport car-park. 'We're drowning in publicity,' he

251

said cheerfully. 'The newspapers have covered the story. Television news picked up the march — or tractor convoy — and even chat shows have featured it. The whole of Italy is up in arms.'

'Good,' said Sara fiercely. 'We must stop Daddy turning the vineyard into holiday homes.' She paused. 'Does he know?'

'About the great escape? I asked your headmistress to phone him.'

'You asked the Dragon Lady?' Hannah exclaimed, impressed.

'Uh-huh.' He stopped at Sophie's car, searching for the keys. 'But all she did was put the phone down on me.'

'She'd be mad,' said Hannah. 'We'll catch it, when we go back.'

'If she lets you go back.'

Hannah frowned, her eyes on his. 'Have we really blown it?' she asked. 'Are we in trouble up to our necks? I warned Sis.'

'But you still came with her.'

'I knew she couldn't do it on her own.'

'Bless you, Hannah,' said David.

She smiled uncertainly. 'So, you'll take our side against my mum?'

'Probably. Then she'll wipe the floor with the three of us.'

'A mass burial's always cheaper,' quipped Hannah.

He found the keys and opened the car, then turned to them.

'Well,' he said plaintively. 'I've driven here flat out to collect you. Then been volunteered as defence counsel in a case we're bound to lose. I'm up to my neck in trouble with your headmistress. Don't I get a single hug from anybody?'

Then he reeled, as he was attacked from either side.

★ ★ ★

'Do I look OK, Bert?' Mary asked anxiously.

'You look fine,' he said.

Together, off-set and in darkness, they watched as the chat show host put the second guest through her paces. Bert felt Mary grip his arm more tightly. Time to reassure — even if he was more nervous than she was.

'Come on,' he said gently. 'You're a professional now. This is your fourth chat show in the last two days, the big one, going out nationwide.'

'Thanks for reminding me,' she gulped.

'Forget the cameras, just focus on the host and your interpreter.'

'Right,' she said.

'That's my line,' he complained.

'Don't mention lines. I think I'm going to be sick.'

'Remember what the set manager said. Head for the chair to the right of the host, as you get onto the stage. It will be free by then.'

'Hope it's not hot and sweaty like the last one was . . . '

'So what? Everybody's nervous.'

'*Signora Kinsella?*'

'Break a leg,' Bert whispered, in the time-honoured luvvie benediction.

'More likely my neck. Can't see in these studio lights . . . '

'Remember to limp,' he said.

'Which leg?'

'The right . . . no, the left.'

Then she was gone. Shepherded by assistants as the host wound up the audience with his introduction for *La Nonna Combattimenti*. A crescendo of whistles and hand-claps, as she limped slowly onto the full glare of the set. She waved her stick, then made a clenched fist for her fans. Cheers lifted the roof. She headed determinedly towards the waiting host.

He bowed low, over her hand. Within two minutes, she had the audience laughing at her first translated aside. Three minutes later, they were her slaves for life. Bert smiled, shaking his head in disbelief: a celebrity, with talent.

In his trouser pocket, he felt the silent

vibrator of his mobile phone.

Edging away from the set, he checked. Kelly: phoning for her routine progress report. The third of the musketeers, there in spirit, if not in body.

'She's on right now,' he whispered.

'How's she doing?'

Bert held up the phone, letting Kelly hear the roars of laughter, the thunderous applause. 'She's a star,' he said, 'fronting our travelling circus. Nobody knows where the column of tractors is now. Nobody cares. The whole of Italy loves your gran. If it's her campaign, then it must be right.'

'So you think we're winning?' Kelly whispered back.

'We're doing fine. But everything hinges on what Dieter finds over in London. Otherwise, we're making bricks with straw.'

Kelly sighed. 'Dieter thinks we're on very dodgy legal ground. But if anybody can get Sophie out of trouble, he can.'

Bert smiled quietly. 'He's a good lad, Dieter,' he said mildly.

'The very best.' Then her young voice became brisk. 'If you see Guiseppe, have him tell the Langhe guys that their wine is selling like hotcakes.'

'That's good,' said Bert. 'They've backed us to the hilt, out on the road.'

'And if you see Dieter when he comes back from London, tell him to phone me and let me know how his research has gone. I feel so useless over here.'

'No. Far from it. You're underpinning the support of the other growers here,' said Bert. 'You're every bit as vital as the march.'

'Doesn't feel like it. And tell Gran I love her.'

'If I can find the time,' Bert said, as another wave of laughter came. 'They're flying us back to Milan, tonight. To the same fancy hotel — unless Roberto has lined up some other interviews.'

'You sound tired,' she said.

'It's your gran I'm worried about. She's running on adrenalin. Doesn't realize how exhausted she is. People won't give her a moment's peace.'

'That's the price of fame,' Kelly said.

'Maybe so. But there are times I wish we'd never started this.'

'Why? You're getting all the publicity you could ask for.'

'True, but it's running out of control, as well.'

Cheers and whistles resounded from the stage. More laughter.

'Sounds as if she's coping fine to me,' said Kelly.

★ ★ ★

At first, Bert thought he had imagined it. He lay disorientated in the strange hotel room, the noises of the outside world blocked out by triple glazing. Blinking grit from his eyes, he tried to stop his heart racing.

Where were they? After a struggle, the name came. Milan.

Then that noise again — the noise which had brought him rocketing out of deep sleep. A groan and a gasp and a mumble.

'Berrrr . . . Berrrrt . . . '

With a surge of energy that left him dizzy, he was kneeling on the hotel bed, struggling to find the light switch. A click. Light dazzled him. He swore.

'Berrrrr . . . '

Mary's eyes were staring wide beyond him. At the ceiling.

There was something wrong with her face. One side, slightly down.

He cradled her head. 'Mary! I'm here. What's wrong?'

He sensed her fight to move her eyes from that fixed stare.

The best she could do, was look over his shoulder. Not at his face.

'What's up?' he asked her urgently.

Another struggle. He saw the lips move, one-sided.

'Berr . . . ?'

'I'm here. Tell me what's wrong.'

His heart was working like a racing-car's engine. It didn't matter.

Then he knew. 'Is it happening again?' he asked.

Her staring eyes finally found his. In them, he read his answer.

'Stay here!' he said, laying her head gently back on the pillow. 'I'm going for help. Down to reception . . .'

In pyjamas, he raced to the lift and slid inside. It took forever to descend four floors. As soon as it stopped, he was squeezing out of it and running over to the old Italian receptionist, who was already reaching for his phone.

'Trouble!' Bert gasped. 'Ambulance. Quickly please.'

The receptionist nodded, already dialling out. He spoke rapidly in Italian, then looked up. 'Symptoms, please?'

'Eyes fixed and staring. Face twisted. I think it's a stroke.'

More rapid Italian. Then the phone was set firmly back on its receiver. The receptionist turned to a cupboard, opened it, searching through bottles.

'Take this, *signore*. Four aspirin. Mix with water. Make her drink . . . it will thin her blood and help, they say. Ambulance in ten minutes. Kinsella, room 423?'

Bert grabbed the bottle. 'Yes. Thanks. I must get back.'

He raced to the open lift, hurtled inside, pressed the button. Erupted from it when it reached the fifth floor of the hotel, and ran towards the open door of their room. Inside the en suite bathroom, he grabbed a glass, filled it with water, dropped in the aspirins and stirred with his finger until there was only cloudy water.

Somehow, he had to get Mary drinking this. He hurried through to the bed, set the glass on the bedside table, and wriggled behind her, propping her head and shoulders against himself.

His panting filled the room. He saw her right hand come up slowly. Pat him gently. 'Ishhh . . . OK,' she slurred. 'Shtill here . . . not gone . . . '

'Sip,' he gasped. 'It's to thin your blood. Ambulance is coming.'

She struggled, choked. 'Oh, sod it,' she said distinctly.

Then, between them, she managed to work her way steadily through the glass. 'Doan' need hospital,' she mumbled. 'Better now.'

'You're going,' he said.

Her right hand came up, covering the hand which held her upright.

'Muzzy,' she said. 'Headache. But didn't
. . . faint . . . thish time.'

'Good,' said Bert, willing with all his might
the ambulance men to arrive.

Down the corridor, he heard the hum of
the lift. Then the swoosh and clank as its
doors swept open. He sensed, rather than
heard, footsteps down the carpeted hall.

As did Mary. He felt her hand grip him
feebly.

'Don't leave me, Bert,' she whispered.

'As if,' he answered gruffly.

★ ★ ★

Twenty hours later, Brian Hargreaves turned
his hired car into the courtyard of Sophie's
villa. His headlights picked out another car,
already parked. He swung round it and
parked beyond, outside the open doors of the
wine cellars.

As his headlights lit up silent vats, he
snorted. These valley people and their
superstitions. Letting the winter in to stop
fermentation. As if the cold — even with the
doors closed — wasn't enough to halt the
vinification process. And so outdated: there
were a dozen varieties of biochemical
additives which would kill fermentation
without affecting the wine.

He switched off his engine, then the lights. Frowning, he reached inside his expensive jacket for his cheroot case. No hurry. Only fools rush in — a danger he must guard against because he knew he was consumed with anger. An angry man was easily defeated.

The oldest trick in the wheeler-dealer's book: get the other man angry.

He lit the cheroot with his gold lighter, drumming his fingers gently on the steering wheel. His instincts were on edge: this whole project was starting to unravel whatever his lawyers said. These latest Italian developments were strange in the extreme. Pointless and irrational. Disturbing.

They shouldn't be happening at all.

He exhaled a thoughtful stream of smoke. It swirled around him in the Mercedes. He opened the door and got out, feeling the sudden bite of non-air-conditioned wind. He had forgotten just how cold these mountain valleys were with the snow-covered Alps in the background.

He prowled around to check the international plates on the salt-stained Audi parked beside him. German. Did Sophie know a German . . . ?

The big man who had claimed he was a lawyer. A claim which was authenticated when his London solicitors were advised that the Sophie Hargreaves case would be defended by a well-known Munich firm of lawyers. That was when the unease started to nibble. Where had Sophie found the money to match his top London team against such a formidable European champion?

The sledge-hammer which had been lined up to crack the nut now found itself facing another sledge-hammer, in the space between.

If the German lawyer was still hanging about the house then this could be a lot more difficult than he had expected. Hargreaves shrugged: challenge brought out the best in him.

But to face that challenge he needed cold air to sharpen his wits. And, more than ever, he must wait until the anger and unease that surged inside him were brought firmly under control. Hargreaves drew back into the cellar doorway. While the wind gusted and sighed above and around him, he was sheltered there. Quietly and unhurriedly, he smoked down his cheroot. He thought through how best to run the meeting — yes, better by far to treat it as a routine meeting than get caught up in it as a personal issue.

Minutes passed while he rehearsed the stages of his attack. Then he flicked the butt of his cheroot into the dark. The broad shoulders straightened and his head came up.

With a final glance at the German international plates on the car beside him, he strode briskly towards the kitchen door. Then knocked.

★ ★ ★

Sophie answered the door.

'Surprise, surprise,' Brian said easily. 'Just came to check out the girls.'

'You took your time. We heard you arrive ten minutes ago. We've been waiting for you.'

'We?'

'Dieter and myself. The girls are upstairs, in bed. None the worse for their adventure, but I gave them a flea in their ear for running away from school.'

A dealer senses chances, miles away. 'Yes, Miss Proctor gave me the rough end of her tongue. But I told her that the fault was ours. And promised to come over and sort things out. We must settle this peaceably for their sake, Sophie.'

'I hope so,' Sophie said. 'Come in. You know Dieter, from your last visit . . . '

Hargreaves nodded coldly at the German. 'The other one? The academic?'

'Up in Milan, with his parents. His mother was taken into hospital last night.'

The old woman who had silently mocked him, Hargreaves thought.

'Nothing serious, I hope?' he asked, with false concern.

Sophie scrubbed her face, with a restless hand. 'Too early to say — they are running tests on her. But she's been doing too much . . . '

Like getting her face in every photograph, Hargreaves thought bitterly. 'May I sit down, please?' He glanced across the table at Dieter. 'Is this meeting off the record, or on it?' he demanded.

Dieter shrugged. 'Your choice. But you have no legal adviser here.'

'True. Let's keep it off the record — for the moment.' Hargreaves relaxed into the hard-backed chair. The ticking of the old wall clock in the kitchen annoyed him — as it always had.

'Right, Sophie,' he said. 'Before we start, what's all this nonsense about?'

'What nonsense?'

'This ridiculous carry-on, with the Italian press and television.'

Her eyes were unflinching. 'Good,' she said. 'You've heard about it, then.'

'Heard about it!' Hargreaves brought himself ruthlessly under control. 'My lawyers received a sheaf of Italian press cuttings from a publicity agent called Roberto Guttieri.'

'He's working for us,' said Sophie.

More alarm bells in Hargreaves's mind. Another professional opponent.

Nothing showed in his face. 'When my legal team translated the reports, they discovered that my name has been blackened and advised me that many of the statements made were actionable.'

Sophie stared at him.

'What are you trying to gain by such ridiculous allegations?' he demanded.

'Simply, to stop you,' Sophie said quietly. 'Prevent you from stealing an asset that you have already given, in our settlement.'

'But there is no settlement,' Hargreaves said. 'That's just the point. It was a crazy letter. It will be challenged by my legal team. Discredited.'

Exactly as Dieter had prophesied, Sophie thought. 'So?' she asked.

'Call off the dogs. Already this Guttieri creature has contacted one of our Sunday papers. Now I can't go anywhere without being stalked by reporters and photographers. I have my reputation to safeguard.'

'We'll call them off, if you call off your legal action,' Sophie said.

'How can I? We need a proper settlement!'

'We already have one,' Sophie said.

'We don't!' Again Hargreaves fought to control his anger: stupid woman, she'd always been stubborn. He forced a smile. 'Common sense, Sophie. Please. If you force me to contest these ridiculous claims, then it's only channelling more of our scarce money into lawyers' pockets. See sense!'

'We might prefer to ask the court to decide just how crazy these allegations are,' Dieter said quietly.

It was the first time he'd spoken. Hargreaves's head snapped round.

'Explain,' he said.

'I've been in London researching your financial background. It didn't make pretty reading.'

Hargreaves flushed. 'I don't know what you mean.'

'You drove in, as I was briefing Sophie. First, we checked back and found that your original offered settlement was grossly unfair. Far from being a fifty-fifty split of your joint assets, it excluded many of your assets, held as shares. You had a whole portfolio of investments that your wife didn't know existed.'

Hargreaves's eyes were icy. 'How did you get this information?'

'Second: after you left Sophie, you went back to your original job as risk manager in a hedge fund. Became one of the leading forces driving for short-term gain at long-term risk. You received huge bonuses, greater than your salary. Taken with your shareholdings, you were several times a millionaire.'

Hargreaves's face was white with anger. 'You do realize,' he snapped, 'that if this is alleged in court, you could find yourself charged with illegal search?'

'We have the paper trail as proof,' said Dieter calmly. 'After the credit crunch, when everything came spiralling down, you found yourself holding near-worthless paper, both as a risk manager, and in your private wealth. Then you lost your job, but got a minor golden parachute. Just as well, because you fell from millionaire to man-in-the-street within a few weeks. Like many others.'

Hargreaves tapped the table. 'All this is irrelevant. In British divorce law, the normal settlement between parties is an equal share of current assets. What I owned and lost is water under the bridge.'

'But which bridge?' Dieter asked. 'What makes you think it will be London Bridge? And a British court?'

'Because that's where disputes are settled between two British citizens.'

'Think again, Brian,' said Sophie. 'There is

only one British citizen in this dispute: the other is Italian.'

'What do you mean?' he demanded.

'When you left me, and I chose to make my future in Italy, I took out Italian citizenship on the advice of my bank. They told me it would simplify my position in law, relative to the land. Everything is so complicated here.'

'So, to summarize,' Dieter said calmly. 'Any claim you have on Sophie's land will be contested here, in an Italian court with its layers of bureaucracy, and its miles of red tape. And you will find that a European court pays more attention to the character of a foreign claimant and what he offered freely, earlier. Then, how he changed his mind after he had squandered a fortune, and decided to come back and steal his wife's land.'

'And our crazy campaign will have everybody watching,' Sophie added.

Hargreaves sat wooden-faced, his mind racing. For once, it could find no quick way out of the mess. 'I shall have to take legal advice on this,' he said.

'Absolutely,' Dieter agreed. 'We are happy to meet your lawyers. In Italy.'

Hargreaves rose slowly from the table. 'What about the girls?' he asked Sophie. 'How will they finish their education if I am left penniless.'

'You are not penniless,' Dieter replied. 'Your final lump sum, which you were going to use as capital for property development here, is still intact.'

'I will look after the girls,' Sophie said firmly. 'With the vineyard up and running now, I can afford to take over their schooling.'

'But Hannah is outstanding. She should be sent to a specialist school, fast-tracked like they do in America. Developed to the limits of her powers.'

Sophie shook her head. 'She goes back to Moorhurst,' she said firmly. 'Let her find her own level there. There is more to learning how to live your life than gathering degrees and medals.'

Hargreaves paused at the kitchen door. Turned as if to say something.

Then shook his head, and left, in silence.

They heard his car engine start, the squeal of tyres as he spun out of the courtyard and set off down the valley road. Suddenly, Sophie slumped at the kitchen table. With Brian gone, all her strength had suddenly disappeared.

She looked at Dieter. 'Have we really done it? Have we really and truly got rid of him?' she asked.

Dieter smiled. 'Until you told me about that Italian citizenship tonight, I had come back to advise you to meet his lawyers and settle out of court. Find money from somewhere to buy him off. Some sort of compromise. But now, the threat of being dragged through Italian courts has changed everything. I think he will cut his losses and run. Go back to what he does best, which is wheeler-dealing until he's turned that last golden handshake into another fortune.'

The smile became a broad grin. 'Sophie . . . now I think it's Brian who doesn't have a leg to stand on!'

★ ★ ★

Outside in the darkness, the wind gusted fiercely. The discarded cheroot flared briefly red, then was blown end-over-end along the foot of the external wall. Another wild gust sent it spinning into the dark of the wine cellars. Then an eddy from another blast spun it round and sucked it back against the internal wall —

— where it lodged against a stack of cardboard packaging. Flat-packs which would convert into cardboard crates, each holding a dozen bottles of wine. David had left them stacked neatly against the wall. Forward planning, for the new vintage of wine which would soon be bottled and left to settle in the storage cellar.

Outside, an uneasy wind moaned round the cellars. Draughts edged round the cellar door. The cheroot butt glowed brightly again. Then dimmed.

Minutes passed.

Then half-a-dozen tiny flames licked up in the dark, running like a child's fingers counting, across the edges of the cardboard sheets.

11

David yawned as he turned off onto the valley road. He wriggled in the cramped Punto seat, trying to find a more comfortable position. It had been a long boring drive from Milan on roads which were thankfully quiet in the wee small hours. Now his concentration was flagging and he was glad to be on the final stretch.

At least his mother seemed better. Her quick and almost complete recovery suggested it had been another of these transient attacks. Not good, but not always resulting in a major stroke. Provided she was sensible. Didn't appear on TV screens each night, as the new darling of the Italian public.

To get her away from people staring, the hospital had transferred her into a private ward. Each time he entered or left, conversation died in the ward. He could see the heads of the other patients and their visitors swivel, hear the sympathetic clucking of their tongues. The son of *La Nonna Combattimenti*. Fame, at last.

It was wearing, adding tension to each day. How his father survived it, he had no idea.

Bert seldom moved from Mary's bedside. He even slept in that chair, refusing to listen to sense or reason: I promised, was all he said.

As his headlights swept over the open clay fields and winter-dead vines which lined every bend on the road, David yawned again. His mind was so full of the thought of crawling silently into his room and bed, that his control of the car was automatic.

At last, he turned through the old stone gates into Sophie's vineyard. He was so numb with exhaustion that he scarcely registered it at first: the yellow-red glow at the far end of the courtyard.

He braked sharply. The cellars. They were on fire.

He could see yellow flames swirling inside, with red and orange clouds of smoke streaming out through the open cellar doors.

He swung the car round sharply to the far side of the courtyard. Cut the engine, and sprinted towards the cellars — leaving the ignition keys still in the lock of the steering column.

The heat was horrendous, beating him back, but he forced himself to stand in the doorway and look. Flames were raging everywhere. The smoke which flooded out around his head was so acrid it made him cough until he gagged.

Starve it of oxygen. He forced himself inside and grabbed the edge of one of the cellar doors. Then yelled. Too hot to hold. He struggled out of his jacket, folded that with hands which hurt, and used it as a pad. The heat from the flames dried his eyes, so that they would barely blink. He smelled his hair singeing.

One door closed. Then, gasping air which scorched the inside of his throat and lungs, he hauled the second door closed too. For the first time, he became conscious of the roar of the trapped fire. Dropping his jacket, he gripped the bolt with pain-filled hands and slid it across to lock the doors.

First job done. He stood gasping. The villa was in darkness. Silent.

People next.

David ran across the courtyard, crashed through the kitchen door, and started shouting even before he was in the house.

'FIRE! FIRE! GET UP! GET OUT, QUICK!' He erupted, shouting, into the hallway and started up the stairs.

'David! What's up?'

A tousled Dieter, in T-shirt and shorts appeared at the head of the stairs.

'The cellar. Fire raging. Out of control. Get everybody up.'

'Can we stop it? The fire?'

David stood, chest heaving. 'Cellar's a write-off. Need to save the house.'

He stood, head down and panting, as first Dieter, then Sara's urgent voice drove out the others. Save the house — but how? Their only hosepipe was in the cellars, but there were buckets and pails in the workshop and the kitchen. Some kind of human chain . . . but how, when they were so few?

'David? Are you all right?' Sophie, leaning over the banister at the top.

'Phone Sergio,' David shouted up. 'Get him to raise the valley men to help us. Then phone your local fire brigade. We need to keep the fire in check until they get here. Hurry.'

'Right away!'

She flew fleet-footed down the stairs, brushing past him.

'Dieter? Everybody up?'

'All here. What there are of us . . . but how did it start?'

'Don't know. Come on, need your help. Buckets of water and a ladder . . . we need to damp down the roofs between the villa and the cellars. Try to hold back the fire until we get help. Then we can maybe tackle the blaze itself.'

'With you,' said Dieter calmly. 'You collect buckets; I will get the ladder.'

'Watch the girls!'

275

'We can watch ourselves,' said Hannah. 'What can we do?'

'Fill buckets with water. Bring them out to Dieter and me. Where's Sara?'

'Getting pails from the kitchen cupboard.'

'Fill anything that holds water — pots and pans.'

'OK,' she said, and flew past him.

David and Dieter raced out, past Sophie phoning in the hall. David hurtled over to the workshop, grabbing metal and plastic pails. Then ran back, to dump them at the kitchen doorway.

'Stay away from the cellars,' he gasped at Sara. 'Doors are trapping the fire inside. Open them, and you'll feed it oxygen.'

Her face was lurid in the wild light, but the eyes and chin were determined.

'Here's two full pails,' she said, and flew back into the kitchen with empty ones. Hannah was already filling pots and pans at the kitchen sink.

'Use the outside tap,' he shouted. 'It shortens the chain.'

Dieter had the ladder already set against the store wall, between the cellars and the house. From halfway up it, he reached down, grabbed the pail which David hoisted up to him. Threw it over the roof, then reached down for a second pail as steam spiralled pink and red from the overheated tiles.

David turned to find Sara struggling out with two big soup pots full of water.

'Use the pails, if you can,' he gasped. 'They hold more water.'

He checked. Hannah was already at the outside tap, which was running full bore. Filling pails and setting them to the side for Sara to ferry over.

'Good girls,' he said. But they were far too busy to hear him.

In the glare of the subdued flames in the cellars they fought their impossible and silent battle. The heat from the cellars was growing by the minute. Dieter, working over the hot roof of the adjacent store, was streaming sweat. In the glare, it cascaded like liquid gold down his face.

Would their water supply hold, David wondered, grabbing pails from Sara and then running over to the ladder to hand them up one at a time? Their panting was audible above the crackle of the flames while Hannah filled and set aside, water splashing everywhere. Every now and then smoke eddied over them, leaving them choking and retching. But still filling and carrying pails.

David became conscious of a swarm of lights streaming into the courtyard, and parking over at the far side. Sergio, and half the valley men arriving. They took over the weary chain and the main problem became how quickly the pails would fill.

'The cellar?' panted Sergio, in David's ear.

'Needs a fire engine. Whole place is up in flames. Just save the house.'

'What caused it?'

'Don't know. It was like this when I got back from hospital.'

'Your mother?'

'Same as last time. She'll be OK.'

'That man has a lot to answer for,' Sergio growled.

In the pauses of waiting for a new bucket to come along the now complete chain, David glanced round. No sign of Sophie. Where was she?

He pulled Sergio into his place. 'Got to find Sophie,' he said. 'See if the fire engine is coming soon.'

He ran into the kitchen, where a sodden Sara was still struggling to fill pails.

'Where's your mother?' he asked Hannah.

'I thought she was with you. Outside.'

He stared at her. Read the same thought in her eyes.

Together, they raced back out into the fire-lit night, choking in the smoke.

Too much smoke. Pouring in a thick cloud out through the half-open cellar door. A door that hadn't opened of its own accord.

David hurtled across the courtyard. Reeled back from the searing heat to trip over Hannah.

'Stay away,' he snapped. 'This is dangerous.'

'You're going in after her,' she said calmly.

'And you're staying here.'

'Wrong,' said Hannah. 'She's my mother too.'

No time to argue. 'Right, on one condition — and it's not negotiable,' David said. 'Do exactly as I say. And stay well behind me.'

'That's two conditions,' Hannah said.

'Who's counting? Lie down — flat on your stomach. We have to go under the smoke . . .' He squirmed through the doorway, shielding his eyes with one hand, while searching for Sophie. She had to be here, and he had to persuade her to get out — and fast, before the vats of wine began to explode.

It took an effort of will not to close his eyes against the searing heat.

Then he saw her, lying on the floor about twenty yards away, the hosepipe trailing from her hand. Her face and hair were lying in a pool of water. Was that good — or bad? He forced himself to wriggle further in.

'Can you see her?' Hannah shouted, hard behind him.

'On the floor. I think the smoke has knocked her out . . . '

Or she was so badly burned, she had fainted. But he daren't think that, let alone say it. However, it changed his plans entirely. While he squirmed in there, beneath the smoke, she could be burning. Or suffocating. He felt Hannah tug at his ankle. In the lurid light of the flames, her face was frightened.

'My hair's burning,' she shouted. 'Take the jacket. Over your head.' And she pushed towards him the jacket he had dropped outside the cellar doors earlier.

He reached back, taking it from her.

'Hannah,' he said. 'There's no time to wriggle in. This is a straight in-and-out job. Go back and fetch Sergio and a couple of others. I'm going in now. But I need people here, to help drag out your mother if I can haul her back far enough.'

'Right,' she said, and scuttled back out through the cellar door.

David wrapped the jacket loosely round his arms and head. Taking one deep breath which felt all fire and no air, he rose to a crouching run and threw himself over Sophie's still body. Grabbed her throat with a hand, and felt. A pulse still there, thank God. But her hair was frizzing as he watched.

He hesitated, then dowsed her hair, face

280

and shoulders with water from the running hosepipe. Then turned it on himself. With hands that hurt, he grabbed her under the arms and began to haul her out. At first, no movement. Then adrenalin surged, and he lurched back towards the door, doubled over her.

Too hot to breathe. The searing heat finally forced him to close his eyes.

Running on willpower, he hauled her deadweight towards the door.

Then got a lungful of toxic smoke, just when he needed oxygen, to stay alive.

David felt himself stumble. Felt the stumble become a fall.

Desperately, with the last strength in his body, he hauled Sophie forward and threw her beyond him, towards the door. Then hit the floor himself.

Rough hands grabbed his shirt and hauled. The material ripped. His knees skinned as they scraped across the floor. He barely felt them.

'Sophie?' he gasped.

'We've got her.' Sergio, his harsh panting filling the world.

David somehow got his feet beneath him and working again.

In a group, Dieter carrying Sophie, they stumbled out from the inferno. Then were blown, head over heels, as the first of the wine vats exploded.

★ ★ ★

David's coughing went on and on until he was retching emptily.

'Give him more water, Sara,' Sergio said.

David looked up to see her face, where soot and sweat and tears were everywhere. 'Your mother?' he asked.

'Got blisters on her hands and face. Her hair is ruined. But she's fine.'

David tried to sit up, take the cup of water from her. Found that his hands were swathed in white bandages.

'Where is she?' he asked. 'Hospital?'

'No, here. The doctor's still with her. Giving her oxygen,' Sergio rumbled.

'The cellar?'

Sergio pulled a face. 'The fire engine got here too late to save it. Two vats went up. The rest are too damaged ever to use again. But you saved the villa.'

David fought to clear his head. 'How did it start?' he asked. 'The fire?'

'The fire chief will tell us. Afterwards. Right now they're checking the storage cellar down below. The workshed, the store . . . every place which was near the cellars.

In case any embers still glow.'

David looked up at his friend. 'And this year's vintage?'

Sergio shook his head silently.

'We could always trade it as mulled wine,' Hannah said. Her black humour brought a twitch to David's lips. That hurt. 'Ouch!' he said.

He felt her grip his arm. 'I was so scared,' she said. 'I couldn't have gone in there. Not like you did. You saved Mum's life. How can we ever thank you?'

'She'd have done the same for any one of us,' he mumbled. Then felt Hannah squeeze his arm.

He looked up at Sergio. 'So we've lost the vintage. And we've lost the cellars. All the equipment. It's a disaster. What is there left to lose?'

He felt overwhelmed. On the edge of tears. Black misery drowning him.

Sergio patted his shoulder. 'Enough,' he said. 'You still have the vines. The goose that lays the golden eggs. And the Old Ones kept you safe, to grow them.'

★ ★ ★

Bert was stretching his legs and hiding from the audience of the main ward when he heard

283

his name being called.

'Mr Kinsella?'

'Here.'

He turned. It was the young woman doctor who was handling Mary's case. Another thirty-something dark Italian, with flawless American, from the conveyor belt of students who had been sent over there for a Master's education.

She was carrying a sheaf of computer print-outs in her hand.

'You've got the results?' he said, his heart in his mouth.

'Relax. It's a good prognosis.' She shepherded him into the empty ward office, obviously wanting to speak to him in private before seeing Mary. 'It shows very little damage to the brain. No swelling. No sign of permanently reduced brain function. Transients seldom do real damage. She got off lightly. Again.'

Her eyes came up. 'Advice — and a caution. I'm going to tell her that there's no call to sit around, put her life on hold and wait for a real stroke to come. There's neither rhyme nor reason in TIAs. This could be the last she'll ever have . . . or the latest in a series. Her blood pressure is good after the early numbers. She's not diabetic — and that helps. If she's sensible in what she eats and drinks, takes plenty exercise, there's no reason why she should ever have another. I'm going to prescribe Simvastatin to cut back on her cholesterol level — that furs up arteries in the brain as well as the heart. And I want you to give her aspirin — I'm prescribing a 150 ml dosage — to keep her blood thin. That should help her too.'

She grimaced. 'Now, the caution. We all followed and enjoyed your protest on television. Local interest, and we liked the personality. But that was *seriously* bad for her . . . the excitement, the heat, the pzazz, the crowds everywhere. Even now, on the street outside the hospital, people waiting for a health bulletin.'

'I know,' mumbled Bert. 'We never dreamed it would mushroom like this. I'd never have let her start on it, if I had thought . . . '

'Sure,' she said. 'Who knows how these things develop? But it's gotta stop.'

'It will,' said Bert. 'Don't ask me how, but it will.'

'She must take it quietly. Live within her problem — and her age. Not fight and rage against them.'

A weary grin showed fleetingly on Bert's stubbled face.

'I'll leave you to tell her that,' he said.

'A lost cause, do you reckon?'

Bert shrugged. 'Of course she's not really like the papers and the television have made out. But they got the truth of it. She's a fighter, always has been. The more you try to tie her down, the more she's challenged. And the better she rises to the occasion. You'll never change her now . . . '

'Wouldn't want to,' smiled the doctor. 'These are survival traits. Just keep her off the television, if you can.'

'I can try,' Bert smiled. 'That's the most I can promise. I can try.'

★　★　★

'One last two-minute gig,' Roberto said. 'And it's all over. *Finito*.'

Bert stared at him. 'Then you'll call off the dogs?'

'Hey, buddy. That's my bread-and-butter you're maligning.' Roberto gestured to the massed ranks of photographers and television crews waiting outside.

'Why can't we just walk out and into our taxi?' Bert asked unhappily.

'Responsibility. To her image, and her public. When *La Nonna Combattimenti* drives off into history, she must do it with a bang and not a whimper.'

Bert glanced down at Mary hunched in the hospital wheelchair.

She nodded.

'OK. But no speaking,' he said firmly. 'I don't want her shamed.'

'Not a problem. No interviews, I guarantee. I'll do the talking.'

'And no paparazzi, sneaking long-range pictures at the villa.'

'I'll do my best. But dammit, Bert, I'm only human.'

Bert glanced down at Mary again. She winked: an old warhorse, scenting gunpowder. He felt lonely in his responsibility. 'May God forgive me, if anything goes wrong,' he muttered.

'It won't,' Roberto reassured. 'This girl has talent.' He leaned over Mary and patted her shoulder. 'Remember your script?' he asked.

She nodded, almost imperceptibly, her eyes gleaming.

Roberto took a deep breath, then said to Bert, 'Right. Just follow me out, then stand back when I take over the handles of the chair. Let's go!'

He strode through the massed ranks of press photographers and television crews, leaving Bert struggling to keep up. The world was full of flashes and whirring cameras, jostling, shouting, cursewords in Italian. With his head lowered, Bert saw Mary flourish her stick. The indomitable warrior, escaping from the dragon's den.

'Now!' Roberto hissed.

He felt the Italian's hands take over the grips of the chair. His head still lowered, he concentrated on being Mister Fighting Grandmother, doing his menial chores. Walking round to the front of the chair he reached down and helped Mary to her feet. As flashbulbs made a thunderstorm he held her steady. Saw Roberto gently tip the wheelchair onto two wheels. Then hold it balanced.

With a final flourish of her stick, Mary turned towards her final enemy. The wheelchair, about to die. She placed the rubber tip of her stick beneath the metal arm, and pushed. Roberto's hands twitched, on the handles.

The wheelchair teetered. Then crashed down. The dragon, vanquished.

The sunlit world of Milan was full of nuclear flashes, and hundreds of people cheering, from the street outside. Nurses and patients waved from every window of the hospital.

Somehow, Bert spirited her into the waiting taxi.

They took off with a howl of the engine

and a scream of smoking tyres.

'Not bad,' said Mary, struggling out of the corner of the seat where she'd been pinned by G-force.

'Not bad?' said Bert. 'The papers will be full of it tomorrow. The Fighting Grandmother throwing away her wheelchair and driving off into the sunset.'

'But it's only morning,' she objected.

'Right,' said Bert. 'Whatever.'

As they weaved out and in through lanes of traffic and reached the motorway, he recognized first the driving, then the back of the head of their usual manic taxi driver from Alba.

'Oh God, it's him,' he said. Then he leaned forward as they streamed past everything in the fast lane. 'How much is this going to cost us?' he demanded.

The driver turned, ignoring the road ahead.

'I wipe away tears!' he said. 'So beautiful. *Bellissima*. I am honoured to be your driver. This journey will cost you nothing.'

'Thanks,' said Bert. 'Watch that car . . . Oooohhh . . . ahead of us.'

Somehow two cars shared most of the fast lane, then they were past, leaving a blaring horn behind them.

'Nothing,' repeated the taxi driver. 'Except . . .'

'Except what?' asked Bert.

289

The taxi driver handed back a thick brown envelope.

'One leetle favour,' he said. 'Just her autograph.'

Bert eased open the flap and drew out a sheaf of publicity photos.

There were about fifty of them, waiting for a signature . . .

★　★　★

With ointment smeared thickly over her face, and her damaged hair hidden under an improvised turban, Sophie was inconsolable.

'Why did it happen *now?*' she asked bleakly. 'Just when we had the wine through all its tests, except the final tasting panel . . . just when our sales had taken off . . . and just when we got rid of Brian, at last . . . we lose a whole year's vintage.'

The acrid smell of burned wood and paint was everywhere, even out on the slopes of her vineyard, with the valley falling away beneath them.

'It's ruined everything,' said Sophie. 'Not just the cellars.'

Sergio patted her shoulder. 'In the valley, we say that you have sometimes to destroy the old to make the space for better things. Your whole future is still in front of you. You have lost nothing which cannot be rebuilt. We have talked it over between us, Dieter and David and myself. Isn't that so, David?'

David nodded. 'Your future rests on your vines, not on bricks and mortar. And your vines are untouched by the disaster — whatever caused it. Once they're pruned, the vineyard is ready to spring to life again. Long before your next harvest is due we will have new cellars waiting for the wine. Trust us on that.'

'We can just about guess what caused the blaze,' Sophie said. 'The fire chief said that the fire started near the cellar doors. Brian was standing there. I saw him smoking a cheroot. How else would these cardboard packs burst into flame? I think it was Brian who did it — but not deliberately. He probably didn't grind out his cheroot butt and that somehow caused the fire.'

Sergio grunted. 'I never liked that man. But we didn't see him set the blaze, so we cannot accuse him. What's past, is past. If Dieter and David re-roof the wine cellar and replaster its walls, the valley men will help you install new vats for fermentation. The three of us have looked. It is a simple task. Take the roof back towards the villa, and check the joists. Replace those which are damaged. New timbers in the cellar, new pantiles for the old.

Two months' hard work will give you fine new cellars.'

'But what will I use for cash?' Sophie asked bitterly.

'That is for you and David to discuss,' said Sergio. 'In the meantime . . . '

He looked up to the top of the ridge, and whistled. Sara and Hannah appeared. Sergio grinned. 'In the meantime, I have two apprentices to train. And four hectares of vines to start pruning. Until David's hands get better.'

Sophie's eyes filled up. She wiped them gingerly, with a bandaged hand.

'Where would we be without you, Sergio?' she asked, a catch in her voice.

He shrugged. 'Hey. You are valley people. This time, Sophie, it is you who will need the help. Maria will look after your house and I will look after your vines until you both take over again. In two months, or six — who knows — it will be my turn to ask for help, or someone else who brings a sick tractor to David. We help now . . . you help later. Just as it has always been in this old valley.'

He beckoned to the girls, who came running down.

'Well? Where are your pruning shears?' he demanded.

Silently, each held up their secateurs.

'Then come. Your vines are waiting.'

He strode off down the slope.

Sophie watched them go, the small figures following the large.

'I want to hold your hand,' she said. 'But I can't.'

She held up her bandaged hands.

'Snap!' said David.

'Maybe I can slip my arm through yours?'

'That's a poor second best,' he smiled wryly.

They leaned quietly together, looking down the valley.

'My hair is ruined. My skin's a mess. I feel like a gargoyle,' she said.

David gently squeezed her arm. 'Your face will heal and your hair will grow back in again. As Sergio says, it is the surface which is damaged, not the soul. It's still the same you, beneath the damage.'

'Very poetic. But imagine having to let my hair grow, so that I can have it cut back short,' Sophie lamented. 'What are we going to do for cash, David? I couldn't face a bank manager now — not like this.'

'I have an idea I want to talk through with you. If you promise to hear me out.'

She looked up at him. 'Have you solved this problem too for me?'

'Maybe, yes, maybe, no. Are you prepared

to take a gamble? On us?'

She studied him quietly. 'I think I took that gamble long ago,' she said.

'Me, too. Look, I don't want to go back to university work. I want to stay here with you knowing that your face will be the first thing I see each morning and the last thing I see each night. I want to help you to make this vineyard and its wine something we can hand on, with pride, to Sara. Because she is the next custodian of the vines. These vines are central to us and both our families. If I sell my house in Dundee, the money we get from that will keep us going until Kelly sells our next harvest. If it doesn't cover everything, like the replacement vats and building materials, we can borrow from the bank. Sergio says he will act as guarantor.'

'Sergio?'

'Don't let these old clothes and that battered APE van fool you. Sergio is a successful small producer. He has been stashing his money away for years. He could buy and sell us several times over. If Sergio offers to act as guarantor the local bank will give us anything we need. He's a major customer.'

Sophie looked down at her daughters, working busily beside Sergio.

'That sounds like a good business proposition,' she said quietly.

'It's more than that: it's a bribe, to persuade you take me in.'

'Why would you want me to take you in?' she asked.

'Because I love you, Sophie. I think I have, from the very start.'

She scuffed her foot on the clay.

'And what if I get it wrong again?' she asked, in a small voice. 'What if I say or do something that ruins everything. Like I probably did before.'

'Then we sort it out, and put it right. You can do the same, for me.'

She looked up. 'We're back to pitching our tent to face the new dawn?'

'Taking each day as it comes.'

With his arms, rather than his hands, he turned her gently to him.

'I can't even kiss you,' he said. With your poor, burned face.'

With a bandaged hand, she touched the left side of her lips.

'That bit here,' she said. 'It doesn't hurt too much.'

★ ★ ★

The knocking at her door was polite but insistent. Kelly frowned. Who on earth was calling at this hour of day? Even Jehovah's

Witnesses took their dinner break. She hesitated, slipped on the safety chain, and opened the flat door.

'Hi,' said Dieter. He towered to the ceiling in the half-light of the landing. 'I brought you some flowers,' he announced. But he made no effort to hand them over.

'So I see,' said Kelly.

'And I brought some wine,' he added, showing the bottle in his other hand.

'You're a bit late for first-footing,' she replied, taking off the chain.

'What is this 'first-footing'?' he asked.

'An old Scottish custom. The first man through the door at New Year, once midnight has struck, brings coal for warmth and some shortbread — so that the house will never go hungry. He shakes the hand of the man of the house. Then kisses the woman of the house. Sometimes he has to concentrate, if he's been drinking, not to get his greetings muddled up.'

Dieter nodded solemnly. 'That would be embarrassing.'

'Don't just stand there. Come in,' said Kelly. 'How did you get here?'

He stood in her hallway, the flowers lost in his hand. 'From Spain,' he said.

'Spain?'

'Yes. I offered to go and collect your

grandparents' campervan. Bert wanted to stay with your grandmother while she is recovering.'

He fell silent, his eyes disconcertingly direct and calm.

Kelly felt her heartbeat race.

'It's a long way from Spain to Dundee,' she said.

Dieter nodded. 'I took the wrong turning at Calais,' he said. 'No, I tell a lie. I had something to do in London. No, that is another lie. I drove past Calais and London and scarcely saw them as I headed north. To Dundee.'

'And here you are.' Kelly had to fight to keep her voice steady.

He nodded agreement. 'Here I am.' The grey eyes crinkled as he glanced beyond her, through to the flat. 'Where is this man of the house?' he asked.

'There isn't one,' she answered. 'But I'm keeping an open mind on it.'

'That is good,' he said thoughtfully. 'We have an old German saying, which I am just making up: it is better to arrive very late for first-footing than not to arrive at all. And we also have an ancient custom, which I am just inventing. I have flowers to bring you light, and wine, to make sure that your house knows love and laughter in the year ahead.'

Then he cleared his throat. 'And since there is no man's hand to shake, the only thing which is left is the kissing of the woman.'

'I thought you'd never ask,' said Kelly.

★ ★ ★

The Italian sun was streaming down, hot enough to split pavements in Edinburgh, Bert thought, without the slightest qualm of homesickness.

'There's only one thing better than sitting in the sun,' he said. 'And that's sitting in the sun and watching other people working.'

'You're sitting in the shade of my umbrella,' Mary quibbled.

'My legs and feet are in the sun.'

'Best place for them.'

Together, they watched the gold and purple of the valley shimmer in the heat, the strange soft folds of the Langhe stretching out into a distant haze. Directly below them was an anthill of activity. The whole valley was here and working on getting in Sophie's harvest. The day before, everyone had been working at a vineyard further up the valley. Tomorrow, it would be the turn of a vineyard almost down at the level crossing. For the last six weeks, the whole valley had been on the move from harvest to harvest as the different varieties of grape had matured.

Bert and Mary, Sophie and David, Kelly and Dieter, and the girls had followed the herd. All as brown as berries, in grape-stained shirts and jeans, sun hats or filthy sweat bandannas wrapped round their heads. Indistinguishable from the valley folk who worked and bantered all around them.

A woman burst into song — as natural as a bird singing.

'We like them singing,' Sergio had growled. 'When they're singing, they're not eating grapes.'

Snatches of laughter, a constant buzz of talk. Italians don't do silence.

Mary sighed in contentment. 'Maybe we should go down and help for a bit again,' she said.

'And maybe we should just sit here and think about it for another hour.'

'OK, you've convinced me,' she said instantly.

They watched benignly from the ridge above the grapes.

'This has to be the loveliest place on earth,' Mary murmured.

'No itchy feet yet?' he teased her. 'No call from the open road?'

'Too busy being happy. Plus, you keep me

busy, moving house.'

'I keep you busy . . . ?' Bert was outraged. 'Whose idea was it to buy the old vineyard down the road from Sophie's? Then give them the land and keep the house ourselves?'

'You said it was a good idea,' she countered.

'So it was — but it was your idea, not mine.'

'Does it matter?' she smiled.

'Not really. Unless I'm getting the blame for it.'

'But that's your job. Getting blamed for things.'

'Now, why didn't I work that out myself . . . ?'

Below them, they watched Sophie laughing up at David. He answered her and dodged. She pushed him and he fell among the vines. They heard his laughter. Saw her throw a cone of dark purple grapes down at him.

'They're happy, anyway,' smiled Bert.

'I've never seen David so happy,' Mary agreed.

'Think he ever misses the university?'

'If he does, he hides it well.'

They heard footsteps coming up behind them. It was Paulo. '*Buongiorno*,' he smiled. 'I don't see much work for me from Sophie, this year.'

'Will it be a good vintage then?' Bert smiled.

'The growing conditions have been excellent. The fruit is in perfect condition for harvesting. Their vines are at their peak, in terms of quality . . . ' Paulo puffed, as he sat down beside them, fanning himself with his hat.

'That was a good thing you did for them,' he continued. 'Buying the Rossi ground and its old vines. That extra land will underwrite the future of Sophie's vineyard — Sophie and David's vineyard. Because, after the harvesting is finished, David and Sergio can rip out its old vines, plough the ground, and replant with new ones. And these new vines will just be coming into commercial production when the oldest of their own vines need to be taken out in a few years' time.'

He smiled. 'At a stroke, you have given them a chance to start rotating and replanting their vines . . . a few acres each year. So that there will always be a core of vines in their prime, and new vines coming through to replace the older ones which need to be taken out. While the people who work the land are doing the same, as the Old Ones watch. Sophie and David, now. While Sara is fast becoming the star pupil down at the wine college. Continuity. As it has always been for centuries.'

He stood up. 'But I must go away. I have a new client to take out to dinner.'

'*Ciao*,' said Mary.

'*Ciao*,' he replied.

They watched him hurry off.

'There goes his latest diet,' said Bert. 'I feel sorry for his wife.'

He waved down at Kelly. She laughed, straightened her back and waved up at them. A wave which changed into a shaken fist.

'I think she wants some help,' he said, half-rising.

'No. Leave them to it,' Mary said. 'Two's company. Four's two too many.'

'Will they be happy, she and Dieter?' Bert asked.

'They are made for each other. Two misfits. Brilliant minds, but a set of values which are out of step with the rest of the world. They will find their niche one day and have a load of fun together in searching for it.'

She always knew, Bert thought. Or at least, what she said was possible.

'Ever wish you were young again?' he asked.

'No. Why? Do you?'

Bert's eyes soared over the golden haze which filled the Langhe.

'No,' he said. 'Not really. Now's good enough for me.'

We do hope that you have enjoyed reading this large print book.

Did you know that all of our titles are available for purchase?

We publish a wide range of high quality large print books including:
Romances, Mysteries, Classics
General Fiction
Non Fiction and Westerns

Special interest titles available in large print are:
The Little Oxford Dictionary
Music Book
Song Book
Hymn Book
Service Book

Also available from us courtesy of Oxford University Press:
Young Readers' Dictionary
(large print edition)
Young Readers' Thesaurus
(large print edition)

For further information or a free brochure, please contact us at:
Ulverscroft Large Print Books Ltd.,
The Green, Bradgate Road, Anstey,
Leicester, LE7 7FU, England.
Tel: (00 44) 0116 236 4325
Fax: (00 44) 0116 234 0205

MS. HEMPEL CHRONICLES

Sarah Shun-Lien Bynum

Ms. Beatrice Hempel has just taken her first job as an English teacher. Closer in age and sensibility to her pupils than to her colleagues, she spends her time outside of school hours reading, writing, listening to rock and roll, and wondering whether she really was right to get engaged. In the classroom, too, she feels 'in-between'. Still young enough to understand her students' way of seeing things, she wants to be their accomplice; but she also feels a terrible responsibility as the adult witness to their adolescent growing pains.